Accidental
Sex Goddess

Lexi Ryan

Cover Design by HOT DAMN DESIGNS
www.hotdamndesigns.com

OTHER BOOKS BY LEXI RYAN

New Hope Series
Unbreak Me
Stolen Wishes
Wish I May

Hot Contemporary Romance
Text Appeal
Accidental Sex Goddess

Stiletto Girls Novels
Stilettos, Inc.
Flirting with Fate

Decadence Creek
Just One Night
Just the Way You Are

DEDICATION

For my mom, who gave me my love of reading, my first romance novel, and the very best example of what it means to be a strong woman.

ACKNOWLEDGMENTS

This book wouldn't have been possible without a whole host of people. I couldn't possibly name them all, but some were more instrumental than others.

First and always, I thank my family, especially my husband, whose tireless faith in me is humbling. He keeps the kids fed and the house from falling apart when I'm obsessing about a book, and he listens to me hash out plot problems the way others might dish out gossip.

A huge shout out to Adrienne Hogan, the world's most patient critique partner, and Annie Swanberg, the world's most awesome BFF. They read this book in its earliest form and cheered me on when I decided to scrap the original and try again. I'm not sure if anything I write would be worth reading if it weren't for these wonderful women.

Thanks to my many writing buddies who lend an ear when I need someone who "gets it." And to my non-writing friends who might not "get it" the way a writer does but support me anyway—I don't know that I deserve you, but I'm grateful.

CHAPTER ONE

"Do you consider yourself a Sex Goddess?"

Reese Regan looked up at one of the most influential women in Chicago and said, "Excuse me?"

Halie McCormack tucked a lock of platinum hair behind her ear. "Do you consider yourself a Sex Goddess?"

Was that a trick question?

Reese chewed on her lip. Was there a *right* way to answer that question when it was asked by the president and founder of Sex Goddess, Inc.? "I…I don't know."

Halie smirked. "Try it on for size."

"What?"

She tapped the brochure in Reese's hand. "The first step of my program is the only step that is the same for everyone. Say it out loud."

Reese squirmed. *Do I have to?* Probably, if she didn't want to alienate the woman who held in her manicured hands the success of the WJRK Charity Masquerade Ball.

"I am a Sex Goddess," Reese said. Wouldn't it being nice if *saying* something like that made it true? *I am a Sex Goddess* or *I am a size six.* Or, heck, how about *I am a size six Sex Goddess heiress with an inheritance the size of Texas.*

"Say it like you mean it," Halie said. "Saying it doesn't help if you don't *believe* it. Try again."

Halie's office grew twenty degrees warmer. Heat crept into Reese's cheeks, and a drop of perspiration trickled down her leg. Oh yeah, she was feeling super sexy.

The programs at Sex Goddess, Inc. were the latest "It Girl" trend in the Chicago area. It was Reese's job to get the company involved in WJRK's next big event—even if it meant doing a pole dance in the middle of a business meeting.

"Sorry. I wasn't expecting—" She wasn't expecting this business meeting to become Sex Goddess Boot Camp.

Halie grinned. "It makes you uncomfortable to say it out loud, doesn't it?"

"Oh, no." Why would it make her uncomfortable? It was only completely awkward. "You just surprised me. I mean, I'm here professionally, and it didn't seem very professional to—" She stopped at Halie's eyebrow raise. "Yes, it made me uncomfortable. Sorry."

Halie shook her head as she walked behind her desk. At nearly six feet tall—five foot nine of which was leg—she moved with the grace of a dancer as she lowered herself into her chair. "Do you realize you've apologized twice in the last sixty seconds?"

"I'm sor—" *Crap on a cracker.*

Halie chuckled. "You have nothing to apologize for. It's my job to point that out. Most women have had their inner Sex Goddesses drowned by society and the pressure of being everything to everyone."

Reese nodded. Probably better that than explain she'd never had an inner Sex Goddess to drown. If she had, it had been a suicide drowning. The note left behind probably read, *"Too inconsequential to go on..."*

"Tell me about your goals, Reese."

Reese forced a smile and took a seat. She was going to be here awhile. This was supposed to be easy—a quick chat to iron out an agreement between Sex Goddess, Inc. and the radio station. But no. Back to square one.

"Each year WJRK holds a charity masquerade ball on New

Year's Eve. This year, we're raising money to support the women's shelter, Almost Home, hoping to raise enough to build a much-needed addition. Sex Goddess, Inc.'s sponsorship of the event would go a long way to help us get there."

Halie nodded. "Very noble, but what about a personal goal?"

Reese stared at the woman—a model-gorgeous trust-fund baby with a Bentley and boyfriend who played for the Chicago Bears. Had she ever had to set a personal goal in her whole life?

"Something totally unrelated to your work. A goal that *Reese* wants for *Reese*."

Halie had done this during an interview with Oprah Winfrey. Question after probing question until Oprah had fat crocodile tears streaming down her face. *"But who* is *Oprah Winfrey?"*

Reese needed a personal goal. Fast. "I'd like to lose fifteen pounds," she said, and—remembering Halie's earlier comment—she tried to sound like she meant it.

Halie frowned and rubbed the back of her neck. "This is the problem with our society. Women think their self worth lies in the size of their jeans or some arbitrary number on the scale."

"You're right." Reese should have seen this coming. After all, she had the inside track on the Sex Goddess, Inc. founder. Halie wasn't going to let her out of the office until she embraced her oversized rear and declared size fourteen was the new six. "I'm sorry. I guess I'm not sure what you mean."

"Huh. Your sister was right."

Maybe inside tracks weren't all they were chalked up to be. "My sister?"

"I'm going to be honest with you," Halie said. "You know Tricia's a good friend of mine, and we talk about you sometimes. I want to help."

"You *can* help me—by sponsoring this auction."

Halie propped her chin on her fist. "When was the last time

you had sex, Reese?"

Wow. She straightened. The words begging to fly off her tongue weren't just colorful, they were DayGlo. "I'd rather not discuss this."

"I'd rather not ignore it. I'm not prying. I'm *helping.*"

Right. "I apologize that my sister bothered you with details from my personal life," she said, searching the conversation for the nearest exit.

"There you go with the apologies again. Do you ever wonder why you do that?"

Reese pushed forward. "I'm really counting on your support for the masquerade ball. What can we do to give Sex Goddess, Inc. the recognition it deserves during the event?"

Halie dropped her hands to the desk and clicked her nails. "Listen, I'll sponsor your event."

The relief that pumped through Reese was better than sex.

"*But* I didn't get into this business for the money."

Better than sex, but just as short-lived.

"I want to help people, and, after talking to your sister, I want to help *you.*" Halie pushed out of her chair. "I don't push my program on anyone, but I'd like you to consider it."

Not a chance, lady. But she said, "Sure."

Halie offered her hand.

Reese stood and took it. "Thank you very much, Halie. This is such a good cause."

"Think about the program. Think about what *Reese* needs."

"Of course. I'll think about it." The lie was so monumental, she was surprised God didn't strike her dead.

"What is there to think about?"

My self-respect? My pride? "This is just unexpected. May I call you Monday morning?"

"I'll look forward to it."

Grabbing for her purse, Reese moved toward the door as fast as she could without running.

"Reese?"

She turned slowly. "Yes?"

Halie handed her an envelope. "The first step is in there,

followed by instructions of how to get the next."

Eat a bucket of snails, run the Magnificent Mile in nothing but body glitter, hang from my toenails over a pit of poisonous vipers—the beginning of a very long list of activities she'd find more enjoyable than completing Sex Goddess 101.

"It's your choice," Halie said, "but imagine how different your life would be if you believed you were worthy of all you desire."

With a sharp nod, Reese shoved the envelope in her purse and hurried out of the office and toward her car. The only rusted nineties-model sedan in the lot, it was easy to spot.

"Oh. My. God," she muttered, collapsing into the driver's seat. She yanked her cell phone from her purse and pressed the speed dial for her best friend.

"Reese! How'd the meeting go?" Mason asked. Her normal perky voice cracked into the exterior of Reese's foul mood, but not much.

"I'm going to *kill* my sister!" She strangled the steering wheel only because Tricia's neck wasn't handy.

Mason laughed. "What'd she do this time? Steal all your sweats and replace them with silky lingerie?"

"Good guess. Try again."

"Hmm…She scheduled you for a boob job without your knowledge?"

"You're getting warmer."

"I can't handle the anticipation."

Outside her window, Sex Goddess, Inc. headquarters loomed over her. Taunting. Today should have been easy, but her sister had turned it into a nightmare. "Apparently, during one of their Girls' Nights, Trish took it upon herself to share her concerns about my sex life"—*or lack thereof*—"with Halie McCormack, and Halie just used our meeting as an opportunity to recruit me into her program."

Silence.

"Mason? Did you hear me?"

"Sex Goddess, Inc. Halie McCormack? As in, the one who you needed for your most important project of the year?"

"Bingo." Reese growled and squeezed the steering wheel. "I'm mortified."

"No kidding." Masey was quiet a moment. "So, are you gonna do it?"

Reese snorted. "Have you seen any pigs fly past your window today?"

***

Ben had Reese Regan on the brain. Which would be acceptable, considering she was his best friend, but the Reese in his mind was naked, moaning, and clawing at his back as he slid inside her.

"Hey, Ben, you gonna play?" Luke called from the pool table at the PitStop. His friend, also the bar's owner, plopped the last balls into the rack.

"Of course." Ben lined up his shot and made a weak-ass break.

Luke raised an eyebrow.

How could Ben not be distracted with Reese on his mind? They'd met at his house for a workout this morning, like they always did, and she'd smelled so damn sweet, all lavender shampoo and flowery lotion. Who the hell smelled that good for a workout? "Damn it."

"I'd say," Luke agreed, surveying the table.

A plan. Anything was possible with a plan. Ben just needed to remind himself why entertaining these fantasies was a disaster waiting to happen.

The three ball spun into the corner pocket and clunked home. "Solids," Luke called.

That was easy enough. First, there was—

"Where's Reese tonight, anyway?" Luke sank another two balls. "I thought she was joining us."

"She said she'd be late. She had a meeting with that Sex Goddess lady."

Luke overshot, sending the cue ball in after the seven. He blinked at Ben. "Seriously?"

"Seriously. But not what you think. Sex Goddess, Inc. is sponsoring something for the station." Ben positioned the cue ball and aimed for a stripe on the opposite side of the table.

Clunk.

He still had it. He lined up another shot and thought carefully.

Reason One: Six years after he'd first decided to keep things platonic, nothing had changed. Sex would mean something entirely different to Reese than it would to him. He sank another ball. She'd be thinking of wedding dresses and picket fences while he'd be thinking of hot bodies, sweat-slicked skin. All she'd want was commitment and all he'd want was to feel himself buried inside her.

"I'm going gray here," Luke complained.

"Cool your heels." Ben studied the table, considering his strategy.

Reason Two: Reese was his best friend, and he had years of good behavior under his belt. He wasn't going to ruin what they had just because she smelled like heaven on a stick and had an ass that made him want to weep.

He lined up another shot and watched, satisfied, as it rolled home.

He was cleaning the table when the bell jangled at the front of the bar.

The air filled with hoots of "Hawk! Hawk!"

"Hawk! Back here," Luke called.

Six foot five, two-twenty, Mark Hawk—tall, dark, and shallow—winked at a girl at the bar, pinched the ass of another, and gave a couple high-fives as he sauntered toward them.

Mark attracted all eyes. Women wanted to be with him, men wanted to be him. Ben wanted to punch him in the face and put him on the fast track to Getoveryourselfville.

"How are Chicago's favorite losers?" Mark asked when he made it to them.

"Good," Ben said. "How's Chicago's favorite asshole?"

Mark grinned. "Oversexed, overfed, and overpaid. I

wouldn't have it any other way." He glanced around. "What are we drinking tonight?"

Mark Hawk, ladies and gentlemen. Highest paid morning drive-time radio host in the Midwest, and still the cheapest son-of-a-bitch around.

"We've got a pitcher over there." Luke waved to the four-top by the pool table. "Help yourself." Luke typically let them drink for free at his bar, but tonight Mark's assumption dug under Ben's skin.

"Is it just us guys tonight?" Mark asked, pouring himself a beer.

"Reese is at Sex Goddess, Inc.," Luke said with a meaningful wriggle of his brow. "She'll join us later."

Mark gaped, so Ben tossed him a bone. "For the masquerade ball." *Which you'd know if you ever listened to anyone but yourself.* When Mark still blinked in confusion, Ben took pity on him, "Sex Goddess, Inc. might sponsor WJRK's Charity Masquerade Ball."

"Reese Regan? At Sex Goddess, Inc.?" Grinning, Mark shoved his fingers in his pockets and rocked back on his heels. "Good girl turns bad. Why do I like the sound of that so much?"

Ben gritted his teeth. "Because you're a shallow fuck."

Mark chuckled and raised his glass to Ben before taking a long drink.

The testosterone around the pool table shifted focus as a tiny blonde wandered over from the bar. She wore tight jeans and a tank that claimed she was TEAM EDWARD-AND-JACOB SANDWICH.

Mark took her in—big blond hair, tight clothes, strappy heels.

"Are you The Hawk?" The blonde gave Mark a shameless once-over.

"Who wants to know?" Mark asked.

The blonde giggled and flipped her hair. "*I* do."

Raking his gaze over her, Mark made an appreciative sound at the back of his throat. The blonde stuck her chest out a little more in response. "Sweet thing, you'd make a weaker man drop to his knees."

"Maybe you're not as strong as you think." Braver now, the blonde crooked her finger through Mark's belt loop and tugged him toward her. "Let me buy you a drink?"

The smile on Mark's face grew as his gaze shifted to someone else. He took a step back, plucking the blonde's hands off his clothes.

Ben swiveled his attention to see Reese. Wavy locks of dark hair had escaped the clip at the back of her neck. Her skirt suit hid every curve Ben had been trying to forget.

When she found their group, she immediately locked eyes with Mark, staring at him like a star-struck fangirl.

Mark winked at Reese over the blonde's head. "Can't do it," he said to the blonde. "The sweetest, most beautiful girl in the city just walked in the door."

Reese's cheeks grew red and that insecure half-smile tugged at her mouth.

Mark abandoned the blonde and extended his hand for Reese, who sank her teeth into her bottom lip.

Ben turned away, lava churning in his gut. He couldn't watch this shit. Reese desperately smitten by Mark. Mark leading her on every chance he got.

Mark wrapped his arms around Reese's shoulders. "Seeing you always makes me smile."

"Said the spider to the fly," Ben grumbled.

"You gonna take that shot or not?" Luke asked, sizing up the table.

Ben sighed. "Eight ball, corner pocket." No need to brainstorm more reasons to keep his Reese-related thoughts in check, not while Reese stood so close making eyes at Reason Three.

"How's the beer treating you?" Reese dropped her purse on their table and came around to stand by Ben. Her hip brushed his and she grinned at him. Ben tensed, side-stepping to put some space between their bodies.

As he narrowed his eyes to line up the shot, Reese closed the distance between them again, oblivious. Ben drew back his stick. As he took the shot, she whispered, "If Mark keeps eyeing me like that, he's going to trick me into thinking a girl like me could actually stand a chance."

The black ball rolled toward the corner pocket then ricocheted. Ben winced.

Reason Three: Only a masochist would go after a girl who wanted his brother.

CHAPTER TWO

Reese was salivating. If she didn't stop staring at Mark and start swallowing soon, Luke's loyal patrons were going to drown in the flash flood.

Reese watched Mark line up a shot. The man was a walking advertisement for testosterone. Broad shoulders, dark eyes, that deep voice that she'd—maybe, once or twice—imagined saying some very dirty things to her. Mark might carry on with his asshole persona from on his shock jock radio show to keep up appearances, but in private, he was sweet, self-deprecating, and charming. Not to mention Oh. My. God. Sexy.

Seriously. Men like Mark should come with warning labels.

Caution: Prolonged exposure to this smokin' bod will leave you hot and bothered.

Ben nudged her and handed her his phone.

Ripping her gaze away from Chicago's Most Eligible Bachelor, she frowned at Ben. "What's that for?"

He nodded at Mark. "Thought you'd like to take a picture."

She snorted and punched Ben's arm, her cheeks warming. "I can't help it. He's eye candy."

Ben grunted.

No, not eye candy, she mentally corrected. The Hawk was sex personified and stood for everything she wanted since

Lance left her last spring. Years ago, as a sensible young woman, Mark was exactly the kind of man she steered clear of. Now, as a recovering doormat, he was the only kind she wanted.

"How was the meeting?" Ben asked.

"Mortifying."

"In what way?" He tilted his glass to his lips.

"She wants me to take Sex Goddess 101."

Ben choked on his beer. "She wants *you* to take Slut Hotness 101?"

Reese rolled her eyes at the guys' nickname for the program that was, perhaps, more infamous than famous. "I know, ridiculous, right?"

On the other side of the pool table, Mark caught her gaze and winked. Lord have mercy, the man was delicious. It wasn't like she wanted to be his girlfriend, but she'd led a really good, decent life, and *just once* she'd like a man like Mark to take her home and use her for hot, dirty, not-gonna-call-you-in-the-morning, drunken sex.

Maybe then women like Halie McCormack wouldn't bring up her sex life in the middle of a business meeting.

Ben was staring at her as if waiting for her to speak.

Reese cringed. "Sorry. What'd you say?"

Ben frowned. "I asked if you were going to do it. The program?"

Laughter burst from her mouth, and then bubbled up again and again until she was breathless. Luke and Mark were staring now, so she did her best to compose herself.

"Oh, God. You're hilarious."

Luke shook his head and racked the balls for a new game. "Reese, you joining us for trivia tomorrow night?"

"I can't, Luke. Sorry."

"Why not?" Ben asked.

Reese avoided eye contact. "No reason," she mumbled.

"Tell us," the men chorused.

"I have a date," she said quickly. She should have concocted a cover story ahead of time. Not that it would have made a difference. She was the world's worst liar.

"Who's the lucky guy?" Luke asked, stepping closer.

Ben narrowed in on her with that piercing gaze.

"Does he deserve a sweet girl like you?" Mark asked.

"Don't know," she mumbled, suddenly very interested in her nails. *Hmm.* That one was short and that one was shorter. *Fascinating.*

Luke chuckled. "You're going on a blind date?"

Reese did her best to keep her expression blank. How had she let her love life become so pathetic that having a date made headlines among her friends? And worse, so pathetic she'd resorted to a blind date?

"Think you'll get lucky?" Mark asked.

Ben didn't say anything, but she could feel his eyes on her. He wanted the scoop. That was generally how that whole "best friend" thing worked, but she didn't want him to know, not when he'd been witness to her *last* blind date.

"Just wish me luck." But she was less concerned about having luck and more concerned about getting lucky.

Halie was right about one thing: She was overdue.

***

"Good morning, Sex Goddess."

Reese settled into a seat across from Masey. "That's me," she said, waving a hand at her workout clothes. "Had to fight the men off with a stick on my way here."

Masey grinned. "I don't doubt it." She flashed a smile over her shoulder to the suit paying for his drink.

At the counter, the man reached for his latte without taking his eyes off Masey. Just as he winked at her, he spilled the drink all over the barista.

Reese shook her head. Masey's sweet smile, blond hair, and Marilyn Monroe curves had that effect on men. Sure, maybe that kind of attention became tedious after awhile, but Reese wouldn't mind a taste of it.

"He's cute, don't you think?"

13

Reese snorted. "Sure. If you like those clean-cut, athletic types with good jobs and amazing smiles."

Masey grinned. "Maybe I'm the one who should be enrolling in Halie's program. She's all about ditching the losers and finding good men. Maybe I could find a guy who doesn't want me just because he thinks I'm easy."

"Oh, Mase."

Mason may have had more than her share of male attention, but she had a pretty bad track record of ending up with guys who wanted nothing from her but sex.

"You know, maybe you should go out with Ben," Reese said. "You're totally his type, and you know he's no loser."

Masey sipped her tea and avoided Reese's eyes.

"What?"

"I just don't think it's a good idea." She waved away the subject. "Maybe we could do the program together. What do you think?"

"You go right ahead. I'll just watch."

"Yeah, it's probably not all it's cracked up to be."

"You're already a goddess," Reese said. "You just need to believe you deserve better."

A barista changed the station of the radio overhead.

"You're listening to WJRK, *The Jerk!*"

Masey grinned. "Maybe Sex Goddess 101 would give you the courage to go after Chicago's most eligible bachelor."

Reese looked at the ceiling where the intro to Mark Hawk's nationally syndicated radio show played. "I doubt Halie McCormack, founder of All Things Feminine Power, would approve of The Hawk."

"So I was at a friend's bar last night," Mark was saying to his co-host, "and you wouldn't have believed all the great pieces of ass gathered in there—just waiting to be plucked."

"Ah, yes, the end of fall brings the young ones back to college, and back to our bars. Sweet, nubile young things. Insecure and desperate for approval."

"God bless them, every one," Mark said.

Masey cringed and Reese shrugged. She'd known Mark long

14

enough to know that The Hawk, his radio show persona, was different than the real man. She'd learned to appreciate his politically incorrect mouth.

"I should get going." Reese took another sip of her latte while Mark waxed poetic about barely-legals in tight designer jeans. "I have a meeting with some of the bigwigs at the station this afternoon, and I have a long list of things I need to get done before then."

"A meeting? Think it's about a promotion?"

Reese bit back a smile. "I'm hoping, you know? I have been there for six years now, and my events are always strong. Besides, my current salary doesn't exactly lend itself to easy living."

Wincing, Masey said, "I feel guilty for letting you buy that condo. I just never thought you and Lance would split."

Me either. "Don't give it another thought. I'm a big girl, and I take responsibility for my own decisions."

"Well, let me know if you want to sell. I don't think you'd make much, but the market is recovering and you could get what you paid at least."

Reese shook her head. She liked her condo. Liked that it was *hers.* Liked that it was in the same complex as her sister and niece. "Let's just wait and see what this meeting holds."

They gathered their things and shimmied their way to the exit through the under-caffeinated masses. The second the door opened, the heat and humidity smacked her in the face, wrapping its damp fingers around her skin and seeping into her clothes. Summer was hanging on for dear life, and autumn couldn't come soon enough.

"Have a good one," Reese said to Masey, hefting her briefcase on her shoulder.

"Chin up, soldier," Masey said. "I bet it's a promotion."

***

Every woman should get the chance to look her ex in the eye after her heart has mended. Every woman should get the chance to meet his gaze knowing her life was better without him, knowing she'd survived his heartbreaking, world-spinning asshattery and come out on top. In said scenario, the girl should be wearing a sexy little black number and have a gorgeous man on her arm.

Reese Regan had envisioned such a moment many times, and as she found herself living it, every essential element was missing. Even the weather was working against her.

"Reese? Is that you?"

Seeing no way out of it, she slowly turned and shielded her eyes from the rain. "Hi, Lance."

Standing under an oversized umbrella, he sported gym shorts and tennis shoes, probably having emerged from the fitness center several yards away. He gave her a once-over, something like triumph gleaming in his eyes.

"Lose your umbrella?"

Jerk. She smiled sweetly. "No, Lance. I was trying to save on my water bill by showering in the rain."

He blinked.

"The rain took me by surprise," she explained, sparing them both her clichéd country song of a day.

But seriously. Worst. Day. Ever.

He looked her over again. "Well, even so, you look really—" He cut himself off with a shake of his head. "You know what? I'm not going to disrespect you by lying just to spare your feelings."

She clapped her hands and gave a saccharine smile. "Aw, it'll be just like old times. Go ahead, Lance, disrespect the hell out of me."

"Still so sarcastic. You look terrible." He sighed as if the fact offended him personally. "And it's not just the rain." He took a step closer and tilted his head. "You've put on some weight since we split, haven't you?"

Dear God, I know I once hoped to carry this man's babies in my womb, but I was young and dumb, and I'd be okay with you smiting him now.

Really, right this instant would be just fine. It's already storming and

16

with a carefully directed bolt of lightning, no one would know...

No? Nothing?

She sneered at the sky.

Lance took another step closer, sheltering her under the brim of his umbrella. "Are you stress-eating again?"

She took a breath. Why couldn't he have been like this when they first met? The condescension, the insults, the emotional abuse—she never would have fallen for him. "I have a meeting, Lance." Now to pretend she was going anywhere but—

"Oh. Shit." He turned and eyed the business fronts. "You're going to Sex Goddess, Inc." A pained look crossed his features. "You know that's not going to change the way I feel about you, right? We're done, Reese. It's been six months. I've found someone who doesn't freeze the sheets, if you know what I mean."

Kiss my ten-pounds-fatter ass, you self-centered— "It's for work."

He held up his hands, the corner of his mouth twitching. "Hey, I'm not judging. I think it's about time you—"

"The station's doing a promotion." Her words were clipped. And to think, an hour ago she hadn't believed her day could get any worse.

"You're still working there? I'd heard they were going to have to—" He shook his head. "Nah, I'm sure it was just a rumor."

Reese clenched her teeth. It wasn't just a rumor, it was the first verse to her personal country song. "Take care, Lance."

Darting though the rain, she headed to the double doors of Sex Goddess, Inc., hair and business suit sopping wet, mascara streaming down her face.

Looking like a drowned rat in an establishment that specialized in duck-to-swan makeovers was her boldest feminist act of defiance since picketing the no-girls-allowed youth football league in middle school. Or it was a pathetic cry for help.

A shiver wriggled up her spine as the air conditioning hit her wet skin.

Do the next right thing, she told herself, commanding her feet to move to the receptionist's desk. "I'm here to see Halie McCormick," she informed the raven-haired beauty.

The woman didn't blink at Reese's appearance, didn't look her over or turn up her nose. She gave a nod and said, "The Goddess will be with you shortly."

The Goddess.

Jiminy Cricket, she'd rather be anywhere but here. The bottom of a bottle of merlot, for example. "Thanks."

She wrapped her arms around herself and paced the small waiting area, trying desperately not to think. She just had to keep shoving everything down until she got through this meeting.

The knot in her stomach grew, ached, and threatened to unravel and take her calm façade with it.

"Reese? Look at you! You poor thing! Come into my office!" Halie wrapped an arm around Reese's wet shoulders and guided her out of the lobby. "That downpour came out of nowhere, didn't it?" she said, closing the door behind them.

Reese put a hand to her damp hair. "I apologize for my appearance." She omitted the part about her broken-down car and her walk in the rain.

Seriously, if she'd had a dog, she'd be worried.

Halie slipped behind her desk, motioning for Reese to take a seat. "Don't give it another thought."

Reese was suddenly glad she'd kept the appointment. Despite Halie's attempts to turn Reese into one of her "Goddesses," Reese liked her.

Returning the woman's smile, she settled into a chair. "Ms. McCormack, I need to begin this meeting by informing you that I no longer officially represent WJRK, though I would like to firm up your partnership with the company for the upcoming charity ball."

Halie pulled back a bit. The air in the room chilled. "What do you mean, you no longer represent the station?"

Reese swallowed hard. It hurt to say the words. "I was laid off." To Halie's quirked brow, she added, "Thirty minutes ago."

Halie crossed her arms and surveyed Reese, eyes narrow. "In that case, what are you doing here?"

Reese dived in. "I no longer represent the station, but the charity event we—they—have coming up is the most important event of the year. I wanted to make sure you would still be signing the final papers." She took a breath and forced herself to stop talking.

"You got fired."

"Laid off," she corrected softly.

"Severance package?"

Reese winced. "One week's pay."

Halie nodded as if pieces of a puzzle were falling into place. "You kept this meeting with me to advocate for the company that just threw you out on your ass?"

"It's an important event." Or at least the cause was important. If Almost Home weren't counting on the money they'd receive from the ball, Reese wouldn't be here.

"Reese, have you given any more thought to my suggestion that you enter my Sex Goddess 101 program?"

Reese gaped. Seriously? After the day she'd had, *this* was what the woman thought was important? "I can't afford your program." Both a convenient excuse and the truth.

"Money isn't an issue. This one is on me, as well as a per diem for clothes, salon visits, and…other necessities."

She blinked. Even the wealthiest Chicago women blanched at the price of the program, and Halie wanted to give it to Reese for free? "That's very generous of you, but I'm only here to solidify your commitment to—"

"Stop, please." Halie dropped her hands to the desk and clicked her nails. "You have such loyalty. Do they even know what they're doing, letting you go?"

Tears surged up, thickening in her throat, and Reese swallowed hard to push them back down. She hadn't yet processed the bomb her boss had dropped on her. She hadn't *let* herself because there were more important things at stake than her job.

"You know, I've been interviewing for a promotions director, but I haven't found that perfect fit yet. Would you be interested?"

Reese leaned forward. She must have rain water in her ears. "I'm sorry?"

"Would you be the Sex Goddess, Inc. promotions director?"

"Um." *Wow*. She was pretty sure this didn't happen in real life. Her ears roared as she tried to process the possibility. Halie was saying something about opportunity and adjustment, something about how change could be good for Reese. "That would be amazing. I—"

"The job is yours." Halie gave a sharp nod. "I'm good at reading people, and you're something special, Reese. I've always liked you."

"I…you…it's…" Words. Words would be good here. But what was she supposed to say? She'd walked into the office unemployed, making a pathetic last-ditch effort to save an event she believed in, and suddenly she was being offered a job that hadn't even been on her radar.

"*However,* I can't have a woman who doesn't believe in herself representing my company."

She flinched as the proverbial other shoe knocked her upside the head. "I believe in myself."

"Should we recap?" Halie stood and placed her hands on her hips.

I'd rather not.

"Today, you lost your job, but instead of going to a bar with your friends and cursing your employer—"

"It's a bad economy." Reese cringed, but it was easier to parrot the party line than let herself be angry. "They really didn't have a choice."

"And you're sitting in a meeting advocating to me on their behalf." Halie looked Reese over—from the damp ponytail at the base of her head to her saturated suit jacket to her beige pumps. "You dress like you hate yourself."

Ouch.

"You do so much for others, and they do nothing for you in return. Even in the bedroom."

Reese's breath left her in a *whoosh*. "Excuse me?"

"Your sister told me about your little problem."

Yep. *Worst. Day. Ever.* "Could we not talk about—"

"I want to help you, and I want you to work for me. But first you have to help yourself." Halie placed her hands on Reese's shoulders. "Sex Goddess 101 will open doors you never even imagined, and I want that for you."

Yeah, but Reese had seen this movie. Take one dowdy wallflower, replace glasses with contacts, treat frizzy hair with flat iron, and place in tight, revealing clothes. Insert into the world and watch her blossom. "I don't think I'm really the type. I'm not like my sister."

It was a good thing she'd been unemployed for almost an hour and not almost a month. Otherwise, she'd probably be falling at Halie's feet begging for the job. As it was, she was kicking herself. If she missed even one paycheck, she risked losing her condo.

But she couldn't pretend to be someone she wasn't, could she?

"How important do you think the station is to the masquerade ball?" Halie asked. "With a good promotions director, could a company like mine could pull off a charity event like that?"

"Absolutely."

"Fantastic. That would be your first project. Because I'm not interested in working with WJRK anymore. I don't like that sexist morning show of theirs. I only worked with them this long because of you. I really like you, Reese."

Reese's mind was spinning.

"Let me know when you're ready. Once you enroll in the program, we'll be happy to welcome you to the SGI team." She scribbled something on a card and handed it to Reese. "I think that is a fair compensation package."

Reese looked at the card and blinked. Silence roared in her ears as she realized an ugly truth about herself: She could be bought.

CHAPTER THREE

Reese Regan, aspiring slut.

Reese wiped the steam off her mirror and contemplated the pejorative term. *Slut.*

Did that mean not having to play the dating game anymore? Did it mean not having to worry if the guy across the table at dinner would be more interested in her cooking skills than her mind? More interested in her housekeeping abilities than her ideas? Did it mean enjoying herself when she was in bed with a man?

If so, she was in. Nothing good ever came of dating, and, frankly, she didn't care for what the old ritual had to offer. Her cell phone buzzed on her bathroom vanity.

A quick look at the display told her Masey was on the other end. Masey didn't know about Reese losing her job, so she had to be calling about the date.

"It's after ten. Don't you have something better to do than check on my love life?"

Masey laughed. "Sadly, no. I want the dirt."

Reese held the phone between her shoulder and ear while she pumped lotion into her hand. "Total bust."

Masey grunted. "Damn. I was hoping to live vicariously through you too. I thought he was a banker."

"Yep, so he had the whole not-a-bum thing going for him, but he spent the entire dinner quizzing me."

"About what? Stocks and bonds?"

"Unfortunately, no." Reese smoothed the lotion over her damp legs and rubbed it in. "Where do I see myself in five years? How many children do I want to have? Do I realize I should have children sooner rather than later if I really care about the well-being of my babies?"

"Nuh-uh!"

"The man actually asked whether or not I had checked in on the health of my ovaries."

"Dear God," Masey breathed. "Date from hell."

Reese took a gulp of her wine. "That wasn't a date. It was an interview for the dubious honor of being the man's wife. He kept telling me how *nice* it was to be on a date with a *good girl*."

"Ew! What did you *say*?"

"I told him I'm not a good girl, I'm an aspiring slut."

"Good for you!"

"I would have said anything to end the game of Twenty Inappropriate Questions. And, anyway, it wasn't a total lie."

"What do you mean by that?"

Reese pulled the towel from her head and wiped the steam off the mirror. *Aspiring slut.* Her hair tumbled around her shoulders, a dark mass of wet waves. If there had been a Slutty Reese buried somewhere inside her, maybe Mr. Banker would have seen that and would have bypassed the questions in favor of a different kind of entertainment. Maybe she'd be acting out some delicious fantasy beyond the realm of her limited—and disappointing—sexual experience.

Instead, she'd cut their night short and come home to wash breakfast dishes and climb into her second shower of the day.

She'd also had most of a bottle of her favorite red wine—the likely culprit behind getting a case of the giggles after the day she'd had.

"I wouldn't mind being a slut."

"Whatever, Reese."

"I'm serious. You know, just for a little while. I'm sick of being the girl everyone takes so seriously. I want a little fun." She picked up her wine glass and took a long sip, closing her eyes as the warmth traveled down her throat, into her chest, and sank in her belly.

"You don't have to be a slut to have fun. You just need to find the right guy. Maybe he's right in front of you and you don't even know it."

Mark Hawk immediately came to mind. She'd had a chance with him once. She'd wasted the opportunity, thinking she wanted something else, but a little piece of bad boy was exactly what she needed.

She always ended up with the wrong kind of guy…or pining after the guy who didn't want her.

"Don't settle for a wild fling when Prince Charming is waiting in the wings."

She snorted. "I found Prince Charming, remember?"

"Lance was no prince."

"He was. He was perfect. The dream. Then one day I kissed him and he turned into a frog." And that summed up her life—a backwards fairytale. She'd fallen hard, moved in with him, and almost destroyed her friendship with Ben.

"God, Lance was such a jerk, but sweetie, he had us all fooled."

Not Ben, Reese thought. Ben had warned her off Lance, and she'd ignored him. She'd even accused him of being jealous.

"We've all been there," Masey was saying. "But not all men are like that, and you deserve better."

She closed her eyes. "Thanks, Mase." Lance had made her believe she didn't. She laughed too loudly, dressed too awkwardly, spoke too much at this party, not enough at that one. When their time together ended, she eventually realized insults were his way of manipulating her.

But one complaint stayed with her.

She was a disappointment in bed.

She frowned in the mirror now. Definitely not Playmate of the Month material. Her breasts were too small, her hips too wide, her belly a little too soft. She worked out, enjoyed it. Regular exercise gave her energy to get through long days at the office. But all the power walking and bicep curls in the world couldn't make her boobs grow, and when she did manage to lose a couple pounds, they came off the parts where she wanted them and didn't budge in the spots she didn't.

Maybe it was politically incorrect, but she wanted to be *wanted*. She wanted a man whose adoration for her was matched only by his primitive sexual hunger.

Rawr.

The doorbell rang, yanking her from her thoughts.

"Masey, I have to go. There's someone at the door. It's probably Tricia wanting to know how the date went."

"Okay, well tell her she sucks at blind dates."

"Right," Reese said. "That and *never again.*"

She ended the call. "Come on in!" She grabbed a thick terrycloth robe from her bathroom door and slid her arms through the puffy sleeves. "It's open!" The robe was dark brown and tattered. Trish would scowl at it, pitch a fit, and threaten—for the hundredth time—to toss it in the trash.

Reese lived alone. Who did she need to impress?

She was holding her glass of wine with one hand and running a comb through her hair with the other when she heard the front door open. She called down the hall, "Do you think Sex Goddess 101 can teach me how to be a slut?"

The laughter she heard was low and deep. And definitely didn't belong to her sister.

She peeked into the hall and, sure enough, Ben stood in the warm light of her small living room, thumbs tucked in his front pockets, smirking.

Cheeks warm—more from the wine than her mistake—she joined him, comb in one hand, wine in the other. "Sorry, I thought you were Tricia."

"That explains everything." He took in her robe, her wet hair, her wine glass. "Bad date?"

"Not a date." Reese scowled. "And calling it *bad* would be an exercise in optimism."

"Care to share?"

"And relive it? Not a chance." She wandered to the kitchen to top off her wine. She frowned at the empty bottle and reached for another.

"Easy there, killer." He was suddenly behind her and putting his hand over hers before she could pull a fresh bottle of red from the rack. "You promised to help with my dad's party in the morning, remember?"

"I want to be a slut." She spun around, abandoning her quest for more wine.

Ben raised a brow. "Well, any more wine and you might—"

"I'm serious. I'm sick of dating. I'm sick of men seeing me as this innocent good girl." She scowled at him. "Why is it that guys assume that just because a girl dresses…*modestly*…just because she carries around a few extra pounds on her thighs and doesn't show her ass, she doesn't like sex? Why do men assume I'm *sweet* and *innocent*?"

Wine sloshed onto the floor, and he took the glass from her hand and set it on the counter. "Who told you that?"

She leaned back against the cool granite. "Just every man I've ever had the misfortune to date."

"And it would be better for them to think you're…" He trailed off, as if choosing his words carefully. "…A slut?"

She poked him in the chest. "Damn—" *Poke.* "Straight." *Poke.* "I'm reclaiming it." *Poke. Poke.* "Men sleep around and they're manly, studly, freaking yee-haw Alpha Males. Well, that's fine, but I'm reclaiming *slut*. What is a slut anyway? A woman who has sex without commitment and"—she gasped dramatically—"*enjoys* herself. I'm sick of men expecting so much from me and giving so little in return." She nodded as if the matter was decided. "Starting tomorrow, I'm going to be a slut."

Ben removed her finger from his chest and stepped closer.

Reese swallowed. The heat coming off his body warmed her exposed skin.

God, he smelled good. When he reached behind her head, she tilted her mouth up to his. She blamed the wine as her gaze drifted to his lips. *Bad idea,* part of her thought, but another part of her—a dangerous part that remembered just how good those lips felt on hers—didn't care. That dangerous part wanted to be kissed.

His eyes met hers, then she heard a click as the cabinet behind her head opened and he withdrew a glass.

She released a breath and he stepped back, putting space between them as he turned to the sink and ran the tap.

He handed her the glass, and it felt cool against her burning skin.

"Drink," he commanded.

She did as he said. When the she drained the glass, he refilled it and handed it back.

When she was halfway through the second glass, he leaned against the wall and crossed his arms over his chest. "Want to tell me what this is all about?"

Reese frowned again. Thought about Mister Your-Eggs-Won't-Last-Forever. Thought about her unfortunate reunion with Lance. "What I *want*," she said, "is a hot and sweaty, never-gonna-be-my-hubby, down-and-dirty fling."

With a sigh, he shrugged and tugged his shirt from his waistband. "If I have to."

She snorted at his exposed abs.

He lifted his palms. "I'm just trying to help a friend."

She smacked his arm.

He grinned in earnest now. "I'll take one for the team."

"I'll keep that in mind. I just want a guy who…likes sex."

"That narrows it down," he muttered.

"I want someone who is more interested in my body than my housekeeping skills."

"That should eliminate a solid one percent of the straight male population."

Reese dropped her eyes to her empty glass of water. "I want to know what it's like to be *wanted.* Part of me—a teeny, tiny, stupid part—wishes I could be one of Halie McCormack's Sex Goddesses."

***

Oh, hell. She was wearing a dress. An innocuous little blue thing that hid every damn curve she had and ended just far enough above her knees to hint at soft thighs and an even softer—

"Thanks for picking me up," Reese said, climbing into Ben's truck, "but I really could have taken the train."

"Don't be ridiculous. We're going to the same place."

She frowned and adjusted her skirt as she settled into the seat. "Well, thanks."

"You need to get rid of that death trap," he said, forcing his eyes off the sliver of exposed skin above her knees. Her POS sedan sat useless in the parking lot of her complex, begging to be put to rest in a scrap pile.

"It's paid for," she said, matter-of-fact. "The mechanic is fixing it this weekend. Besides, I use the L most of the time. What do I need with some fancy car?"

Right, and she couldn't afford a car payment since that asshole ex of hers had convinced her they should buy a condo together. Then he'd left and stuck her with the mortgage.

If she'd take Ben up on his offer to let her live with him, she'd be able to sell the condo and buy a reliable vehicle.

"Well, it works most of the time."

He turned back to her and quirked a brow. "*Most* of the time? That puts my mind at ease, Reese. Here I was worried it might break down on you in the middle of rush hour on I-90, but now that I know it works *most* of the time, I'll put it from my mind."

"You worry too much, but you don't need to. Everything's going to work out." Her eyes widened as she spotted two cups of coffee on the console. "Is one of those for me?"

Her dark hair was pulled into a high ponytail, exposing the smooth skin of her neck and reminding him of the freshly bathed, wine-flushed Reese he'd found in her apartment last night. He couldn't stop picturing the way her robe had started to slip off her shoulders, or the way she'd looked at him—if only for a moment—when he'd stepped close.

He couldn't stop wondering what the fuck was wrong with him.

Ben forced his gaze away from her as she sipped the coffee. But she made soft little moans of pleasure with each sip, and he had to squeeze the steering wheel to keep from staring, to keep his brain from imagining those moans in a completely different context. "I assume you've moved past your drunken *I want to be a slut* plans."

"Oh, I haven't moved past it," she said. "I just know better sober than to believe I can do it. I'm not Sex Goddess material."

He snorted. Was she really so naïve?

She shrugged. "Life goes on."

"Thanks for doing this," he said gruffly, changing the topic to something safer.

She reached over and squeezed his thigh, just above his knee, and left her hand there. "I'm happy to. I owe a lot to your parents."

He pulled onto the road, heading north of the city to his parents' house. Months ago, he'd asked Reese to help him with preparations for his dad's retirement party. She was good at that kind of thing after all. But now all he could think was if he put the party together by himself, he wouldn't be sitting here wanting her so damn much.

She squeezed one more time before pulling her hand away, and his cock strained uncomfortably against the fly of his jeans.

"When's everyone supposed to get there?" she asked.

He cleared his throat. "Noon. Are Trish and Sydney going to make it?"

Reese frowned and leaned back in her seat. "Yes," she grumbled. "God, I really don't want to talk to my sister right now, but it will be good to see Sydney. Do you know she's playing piano in the high school jazz band?"

"You mentioned it. Like twelve times."

"She's in eighth grade. Forgive me for being a proud aunt."

Ben shot her a look before returning his focus to the road. "Why don't you want to talk to Trish? Because of the date?"

"The date was terrible," she said, "but she meant well. But I can't believe she told Halie McCormack—" She cut herself off and her eyes went wide.

"What'd she tell her? They're friends, right?"

"She just—" She shook her head again, and from the corner of his eye, he could see her cheeks flushing. "She's the one who made Halie think I need Sex Goddess 101."

Ben narrowed his gaze. "You're not telling me something."

"It's personal," Reese grumbled behind her coffee.

He grunted. "Never stopped you from sharing before."

"It's embarrassing. But maybe everything happens for a reason. Something good might come of it."

"Come on, Reese. It's me. Your buddy. The guy who saved you from what probably would have been a nasty hangover. The pal who came to your rescue when your car wouldn't start *again*."

"You don't want to know."

"I really do," he promised. "Anyway, I'm a little hurt that you'd trust Trish with this information and not me."

She shook her head again, cheeks crimson.

As he pulled onto the interstate, he dropped it. For now.

***

Satisfaction filled Reese as she looked around the party. The guests had arrived in droves to celebrate the long and successful career of Thaddeus Hawk, owner and founder of Hawk Construction. The coolers were brimming with drinks, the tables were filled with food, and the Hawk brothers were working the grills.

"It's so nice to see you, sweetie," Caroline Hawk said, pulling Reese into her large, soft body for a hug. "When you were dating that bad man, we did not see you nearly enough."

"That bad man" was what Caroline had called Lance.

Reese made a face. "I'm sorry about that." Lance hadn't believed it appropriate for Reese to spend so much time with another man's family, even if they had treated her like one of their own for so many years. Had she really been so stupid?

Caroline patted Reese's shoulder before pulling away. "Well, that's all behind you now."

Gratitude and regret and love all swirled together and grew thick in her throat, so Reese only nodded in reply.

Someone called across the lawn and Caroline squeezed Reese's hand before sliding away.

"The party looks great!"

Reese turned to see Trish, bright red hair bouncing at her jaw line, green eyes bright. Her sister was a beauty in the league of Halie McCormack. Which was probably why they spent so much time together. Beautiful people always flocked to each other like that. But unlike Halie, Trish hadn't had the world handed to her on a platter.

"Thanks," Reese finally replied. "I didn't really do much, but I know it made Ben feel better to have me here. Where's my beautiful niece?"

"She's inside," Trish said, "fondling the Hawks' baby grand, where else?"

Reese grinned. "I told Caroline about the jazz band—she's very impressed."

"You told everyone about the jazz band."

Shrugging, Reese said, "It's a big deal."

"So." Trish clapped her hands. "How'd the date go?"

Reese stuck out her tongue and pointed her thumb to the ground.

"Really?" Trish screeched. "Man, he seemed so solid too, really ready to settle down."

"Next time, less solid, more manwhore, okay?"

Laughter bubbled out of Tricia's lips, making Reese grin.

"I'm serious. I'm not looking for that kind of…intensity right now. After Lance, I deserve a little fun."

Tricia's face grew serious. "Of course you do. Damn. You and I know how to pick 'em, don't we?" She shook her head. "I'll do better next time."

"No more blind dates, though," Reese said. "If you want me to meet someone, introduce me. That blind date stuff is just hellacious."

"Old-fashioned introduction to a manwhore. Got it."

Reese took a deep breath, casting a glance around to make sure they were speaking in relative privacy. "You shouldn't have told Halie."

"Told Halie what?"

Reese cocked her head. "Really? You expose my biggest secret to the queen of sexual pleasure and you don't *remember*?"

Slowly, realization dawned and Tricia's eyes grew wide.

"She brought up my little...*problem* during our business meeting. Do you know how awkward that is?"

Trish covered her mouth with her hand. "I'm sorry. It just came out." Her shoulders slumped. "You must hate me."

"You're my sister. I can't hate you. I should, but I can't." She adjusted a vase of flowers on one of the many tables set up around the yard. "Oh well, it's probably thanks to that little tidbit that she took pity on me and offered me a job."

Trish looked confused, so Reese filled her in on her Friday from hell, from the lay-off to the job offer.

"Wow! You get to do Sex Goddess 101 for *free*?"

Reese groaned. "You're missing the point. It's a *job*. A great one."

"Halie's amazing. I can't wait to see what she does for you."

A sick knot grew in the pit of Reese's stomach. She preferred to focus on the job, not the embarrassing reality that she was going to have to become one of the illustrious Sex Goddesses. "At least one of us is excited," Reese muttered.

"In the meantime, I'm going to find you that manwhore you want so badly."

Reese's gaze unconsciously settled on the Hawk brothers at the grill.

Trish giggled as she saw where Reese was looking. "Mark Hawk? Oh, God, Ben would kill me."

Mark caught her eye and winked.

Was she an aspiring slut or not? "What Ben doesn't know can't hurt him."

CHAPTER FOUR

Ben turned away from the grill at the sound of laughter and spotted Reese and her sister chatting a few yards away. Whatever big secret Tricia exposed must not have been too important, because Reese's big eyes were bright with humor.

Something squeezed in his chest at the sight of her smile. It made her—

Next to Ben, Mark made a *tsk*ing sound. "Keep looking at her like that, and she's gonna figure it out."

Ben frowned. "Figure what out?"

He gave Ben a knowing look. "Come on, man, you've been making eyes at her since that dude she was dating moved out of her place."

"I haven't." He cleared his throat. "It's been nice having her back in my life again. Lance was possessive as all hell."

"I don't really see what's stopping you."

You, asshole. "Nothing's stopping me from anything. We're friends." He jammed his hands into his pockets. He and Reese had agreed years ago that neither would ask for more. Was he the genius who'd thought of that?

Mark rubbed his chest thoughtfully. "Yeah, it's probably not the time to rock the boat. She needs friends right now. That's some shit, what the station did to her." He turned back to the grill and flipped a few burgers. "I swear that place is run by a bunch of idiots."

Ben froze. "What?"

"I'll admit I think she can do better. Staying at the station was the easy choice, so maybe this will turn out for the best."

Ben didn't hear the rest because he was striding through the lawn toward Reese.

He stalked up to her and took her by the arm, and the smile on her face froze.

"What's going on?"

He maneuvered his way through the guests, making his way to the back door. When he pulled her into his parents' house, he found the closest private room.

"Ben," she said as he shut the door, "why are we in the bathroom?"

"You lost your job?"

She lifted her chin. "I did."

"Why the hell didn't you tell me?"

"I think we both know the answer to that."

He took a step toward her, and she backed against the vanity. "Then you'd be wrong because that seems like information you'd share with *your friends*."

"I don't want you sweeping in to the rescue. I don't want you paying my mortgage or filling my tank. I don't want any of the things you like to offer when I find myself in a pinch."

He crossed his arms. "That's what friends do."

"Okay, then let me ask you something. When you found out, how many seconds later did you decide I should sell my condo and move in with you?"

Ben opened his mouth to reply, then closed it. She knew him too well, but that didn't mean it wasn't a perfectly reasonable plan. It was a good plan now, and it had been a good plan when Lance left her. "You never had money problems before you bought that place."

Her lips quirked. "I don't think that's really why you hate my condo so much."

"What do you mean?"

"Never mind. It's a non-issue."

"How do you figure?"

"I was offered a job yesterday."

He raised a brow. "Another piece of information I'd think I wouldn't be the last to know."

"You're not the last to know." She blew out a breath. "I haven't accepted yet. Sex Goddess, Inc. needs a promotions director."

The words washed away his irritation. "Really? And the job is yours? It's a done deal?"

"The job is mine," she continued, "on the condition that I complete Sex Goddess 101."

Ben grinned. "You're going to do the Slut Hotness 101 program?"

"Don't call it that," she said, slugging him in the arm.

Even as he rubbed the dull ache, he couldn't help the laughter in his voice. "But it's a condition of getting the job? The job that's going to save the overpriced condo you're so determined to keep?"

She dropped her shoulders. "I don't know what I'm going to do." Her brow wrinkled and defeat pulled at her features.

Shit. "Hey…" He tilted her chin up so she'd look at him. "It's going to be okay."

She cocked her head. "Yeah? Ben, you know me better than anybody and you laughed at the idea. I'm not cut out for this. I can promote the hell out of it. I know I can. But I can't do it. Me? A Sex Goddess? Seriously, can you picture that?"

You have no idea. "Fake it," he said with a shrug. When she scowled, he grabbed her hands and squeezed. "I'm serious, Reese. It's five steps, right?"

"Ten."

"Okay, so you'll do ten things, pretend you're one of her Slut Hotness converts, and you'll have the job of your dreams." He shrugged again. "Fake it."

She took a deep breath and some of the tension left her face. "Are you sure you're not just saying this so you can see me wear skimpy clothes?"

"It's an added bonus."

She sighed and leaned her head against his shoulder. "Thank you, Ben."

He shut his eyes, resisting the urge to pull her body close. "Sure thing."

Tucking his chin, he buried his nose in her hair, taking a hit of her scent, that soft and feminine smell that haunted him.

She drew away. "You seem different lately. Is something wrong?"

"Work stuff is getting to me." And it was the truth, if only part of it. "I have big plans and Dad—" He cut himself off with a shake of his head. He didn't want to talk about Hawk Construction right now. He didn't want to talk about anything. He wanted to keep her in his arms as long as he could get away with it.

She studied him silently for a minute. "You want more," she said simply.

She had no idea. And for the first time since he had knocked on her door six years ago, Ben let himself consider the possibility of taking what he wanted.

***

The gorgeous creatures surrounding Reese didn't need Sex Goddess Boot Camp. They needed a mirror.

"Can we leave now?" Reese asked Mason as they entered the convention center and joined the masses of women milling around, waiting to be transformed.

"Chin up, soldier. We're doing this thing."

One week ago today, Ben had solved her Sex Goddess dilemma by telling her to fake it, and now she was here, ready to dive in to the biggest fake-out of her life, grateful to have Mason by her side. Halie had encouraged her to bring a friend to Sex Goddess Boot Camp, citing better success rates for women who go through the program with a friend.

How did one measure success of a program like this? Number of jaws dropped? Number of one-night stands?

Reese eyed the women around her and felt her own attractiveness drop exponentially. Some lithe, some curvy, some blonde, some brunette, one even sporting purple streaks in her platinum 'do—every one of these women was beautiful. Reese might not know the designer name brands, but she recognized expensive clothes when she saw them. Of course, with a weekend at Sex Goddess Boot Camp running nearly a thousand dollars—more for those who would continue on with SG 101—the experience attracted the kind of women who could afford nice clothes.

"Did you remember to bring your five most flattering outfits?" the woman at the registration desk asked.

Reese hefted her garment bag onto the table and took a breath. She could do this. "I hope they're okay."

The woman waved a hand dismissively. "It doesn't really matter. It's a *learning opportunity.* Now go on in, the Goddess will be with you shortly."

Reese and Mason exchanged a look.

"Are you going to have to call her that when you work for her?" Mason asked in a whisper.

Reese shook her head. "I couldn't. Not with a straight face."

They wandered into the gymnasium and were ushered into a line of women standing in front of the bleachers.

Reese made fists to keep herself from fidgeting.

"My, oh my, there is some *sexy* going on in here!" Halie McCormack strode into the room, all long legs, high heels, and thousand-watt smile.

A cheer rose up as she positioned herself in front of them. Some women clapped. Some jumped up and down. Reese just wanted to leave.

Halie motioned for the crowd to quiet. "Being a Sex Goddess isn't simple, but the rules are." She paced back and forth in front of her recruits, hands clasped behind her back.

"The first rule of Sex Goddess Boot Camp," Reese said under her breath, "is you do not *talk* about Sex Goddess Boot Camp."

Masey snorted, earning her a glare from their fearless leader.

"Rule one." She stopped in front of a redhead and yanked the tie from her hair, sending a cascade of thick red hair down her back. "Ponytails are for workouts and housework. Nothing else. No exceptions."

The redhead nodded enthusiastically and shook out her hair in a frenetic rush of movement.

Reese reached for her own hair tie and pulled it out as inconspicuously as possible.

"Rule two," Halie shouted, putting two fingers in the air. "You will wear clothes that fit you and flatter your body." She sent a meaningful glance in Reese's direction.

"Ouch," Masey muttered.

Reese huffed softly. "No kidding."

"Rule three…" she said, pausing dramatically to look each recruit in the eye. "You will seek opportunities to give and receive pleasure."

Hoots of agreement filled the gym and Reese eyed the door.

Masey nudged her. "Don't even think about it."

"Rule four," Halie called, "—and this is what it's all about—you will reach for the life you want, not the life that you've been given. You will reach out and make it happen because you *deserve* it.

"Now, let's get this party started! Sex Goddess Boot Camp isn't just a weekend conference," Halie said. "It's the first day of your new life. It's a life of fulfillment and excitement. And it's available to *every* woman!"

The crowd roared in approval. Reese was seriously questioning her judgment.

"Are you ladies ready to experience the most important weekend of your life?" Halie's voice was serious now.

Pre-orgasmic affirmations of "Yes, yes!" filled the room.

"Are you ready to take control of your future?"

More cheering, a few whistles, and even an old-school Arsenio Hall-style "Woof! Woof!"

"I'm going to be asking you a lot of questions this weekend. Let's start with a few basics." Halie looked around the now-quiet room. "When was the last time you felt manipulated into doing something?"

Oh, the irony, Reese thought.

Halie pointed at the redhead.

"Last week."

"What happened?"

"I went out on a date with this guy I wasn't interested in because he gave me this sob story about being lonely. It was horrible, and I had to call a friend to rescue me because I could tell he was going to guilt me right into his bed."

"That's not okay," Halie said. "Don't waste your time with people who don't bring you joy. Say it with me, ladies: *Never again.*"

"*Never again,*" they chanted, and at least Reese could join in on that one with sincerity.

"When was the last time you felt sexually *powerful?*" Halie asked, then pointed at Reese. "Reese, you first."

Reese froze. "Excuse me?"

"You have sexual power. When was the last time you felt like a goddess in a man's arms?"

She swallowed and tried to think of any answer except the one that came to mind.

"Don't over think it," Halie said. "The first answer that comes to mind is the most honest."

Honest. Okay... "Once, someone came to my apartment at ten o'clock at night just because he wanted the chance to kiss me. I didn't expect it."

"Beautiful. What was this guy's name?" Halie asked.

Reese flashed a look at Masey before she admitted, "Ben Hawk."

***

"Good morning!" a sing-songy voice called from Ben's front door.

Ben stood in the middle of his kitchen, sipping coffee and attempting to unglue his eyelids.

Reese strode into the room, her presence kicking his brain into gear better than a whole pot of coffee.

She wore a white tank, yoga pants that clung to the curve of her ass, and a smile way too sunny for a Monday morning.

Not for the first time, Ben imagined she wasn't joining him fresh from her car but that she was joining him from his bed. She wouldn't be wearing workout clothes but maybe one of his old t-shirts. She'd pad toward him in bare feet, cotton brushing the tops of her thighs, and she'd wrap her arms around his neck with the smile of a recently satisfied woman. He would slide his hands under her shirt and cup an ass cheek in each hand as he put his mouth on hers. Then they'd get a whole different kind of workout.

A dangerous fantasy. In the real world, Reese smacked a kiss to his cheek like she was greeting her little brother. To add insult to injury, she stole his mug out of his hands and took a gulp of his coffee. The soft moan of pleasure that escaped her lips played all too well into the images flashing through his mind. So did the way she closed her eyes and tilted her head back, pleasure running across her face.

Jesus. Ben tried to get a handle on himself, but, hell, he was only human, and Reese enjoyed a sip of coffee in a way that made a man think of slow, sweaty, *thorough* sex.

How was he supposed to avoid imagining the expression on her face as he teased her breasts? What sounds would she make when he ran his tongue across a hardened nipple? And when he ran his mouth down her stomach and tasted her between her legs, what sounds would she make then? Would she quietly open her legs for him? Or would she cry out in pleasure, tug on his hair?

She cocked her head, studying him but not seeing him. Reese saw a friend when she looked at him, not a man. And maybe for a while he'd only seen a friend when he'd looked at her. That was all he'd let himself see. But at some point he'd let his guard down, and now when he looked at Reese he didn't just *see*. He *wanted*.

"Have a lot on your mind this morning?" she asked.

He nodded slowly, let his fingers brush over hers as he took his mug back. "You could say that." He slugged back the rest of his coffee and headed toward the basement without preamble. Reese followed, humming softly under her breath, a sound low enough to slingshot his mind straight back to his fantasy, to the idea of her body under his hands. His mouth.

"Hey, grumpy," she said when they reached the bottom of the stairs. She tugged on his shoulder until he turned to face her. "Anything I can do to improve your mood this morning?"

"I can think of a few things." He couldn't help himself. He let his gaze travel slowly down her body, lingering at her curves. His gaze traveled so slowly back to her face, he had enough time to picture every inch of her bare, exposed, ready for him. It was an image that was half fantasy and half memory.

When he returned his eyes to her face, a deep red blush stained her cheeks. "Ben!" She landed a soft punch to his solar plexus.

Ben lifted a shoulder in a half shrug. "You asked."

"When was the last time you got laid?"

He knew down to the day, but he wasn't about to share the truth with Reese—not when the date was just as significant in her life. "A few months."

"Well, you need to do something about that."

"You volunteering?"

CHAPTER FIVE

"Spill," Masey demanded an hour after Reese had finished her workout.

The Coffee Spot hummed with activity. Classic rock played lightly overhead and caffeine addicts milled around the counter, casting evil glances toward anyone who dared get between them and their next fix.

Reese did her best to look innocent. "Spill what?"

"Yesterday you said you'd made out with Ben. I want details."

"I said he came to my apartment to kiss me."

"Spill."

"I'd rather not."

Reese frowned at the sealed envelope she'd pulled from the depths of her purse. The boot camp wasn't anything like what she'd expected. There'd been no makeover, no tips on how sway her hips when she walked, not even a lesson on perfecting her blowjob. Instead the whole day had been an exercise in introspection, reflection, and self-evaluation.

Reese had actually…enjoyed it. Everything except the moment at the beginning when she exposed her secret history with Ben.

"Was this recent?" Masey asked. "Like since you broke up

with Lance?"

That jolted Reese out of her reverie. "No! No, it was…" She smudged a drip of coffee with her thumb. "It was before he and I became friends."

Masey leaned back in her chair and studied Reese. "Well, well, well. And here I thought the second you two gave in and touched each other, the rest would be history."

"What? Why would you think that?" Damn. She hated this. Learning to give a pornstar-caliber blowjob wouldn't have sucked this much.

"Reese, everyone can see—"

"We're. *Just. Friends.*" She ground the words out through her teeth, then forced herself to relax her shoulders. "That's all."

Masey nodded, but Reese got the impression she was humoring her more than believing her.

"Listen." Reese took a deep breath. "I'm not stupid. I know everyone thinks we're together or going to get together, but it's not like that." She swallowed the lump in her throat and shrugged. "I tried. He didn't want me."

The sympathy on Masey's face was enough to make Reese want to run away.

"We decided the only way to salvage our friendship was to agree that neither of us would ask for more than friendship from the other." She forced a smile, but the memory was anything but happy. "The rest is history."

"I'm sorry, Reese," Masey said. "I had no idea, but I just don't understand. You said, he came to your apartment because…"

Her coffee sloshed and she winced. "I don't like to talk about it."

"Okay. Is there a reason you haven't opened that yet?" Masey pointed to the envelope in Reese's hands.

"Chicken?"

"Pretty much." Reese tapped the envelope on the table, grateful to escape the interrogation about her and Ben's past. "Step one is the same for everyone, right? It can't be that bad."

"Open it."

Reese handed it to Masey. "You do it."

Masey didn't hesitate. She tore into it and withdrew the letter inside. "Step one," she read, "say it out loud."

"IamaSexGoddess," Reese said just loud enough for Masey to hear. "Now, what did she mean by giving me instructions for getting the next step?"

Masey laughed, a big, contagious sound that filled a room and made anyone with an ounce of heart smile. "You're not getting off that easy. There's more." She handed the note to Reese.

Step One: Say it out loud. Declare your intent to the Universe!

Dear Reese,
I am so pleased that you're choosing to embark on this journey with me.

"More like she conned me into it," Reese grumbled, but she couldn't be too sour about it. The woman was giving her a fantastic job, after all.

I know you're scared, and right now you may not even believe in my program.

She looked up. "That's not true. I totally believe she can transform me in ten steps."

Masey crossed her arms, doubt compressing her features. "You do?"

"Yes! I also believe in that an obese geriatric can fit down a chimney, leave the exact kind, type, and number of gifts the child's family can afford, and fly his reindeer off the roof all without making a sound."

Masey's lip twitched. "Just read the letter."

Belief will come with time. With each step you'll see changes in yourself that will motivate you to continue.

Write me a letter describing the Sex Goddess version of Reese. Spend some time fantasizing first, then write it down.

"Damn," Reese muttered. She looked at Masey. "I'm dead, aren't I? I'm dead and in hell for having impure thoughts about the Hawk brothers."

Masey wriggled her brows. "Brothers, plural? So you admit it?"

Reese's cheeks burned but she smiled. "Look at them. Who hasn't?"

"No one with working mommy parts, I'll grant you that."

Reese sighed. "I don't know what I've gotten myself into, Mase."

"Buck up, soldier. You can do this."

"Right." Reese took a sip of her caramel latte. She'd expected Sex Goddess 101 to put women on strict no-carb diets and exercise regimens, but Halie had made it very clear during yesterday's boot camp that their goals shouldn't include weight loss.

"Aren't you excited?" Masey asked.

"Oh, Masey, always the optimist. I'm mortified. This is exactly the kind of thing a girl like me avoids."

"What do you mean *a girl like you*?"

Reese waved away the question. "I should get going. Need to make a good impression on my first day. Maybe if I'm an awesome employee, she'll keep me when I am a miserable failure at her program."

"Come on, it's only ten steps," Masey said. "And you're half Sex Goddess already."

"Ten steps," Reese repeated. "How hard could it be?"

***

"It's not an easy program," the leggy blonde told Ben. Holly? Hadley? Hell if he could remember the name of the woman who had shown up to his worksite unannounced.

Ben's crew dragged another set of ancient cabinets out of

the house, slowing when they spotted the platinum blonde. He couldn't blame them. The woman was sex on ice. A serious face on a body poured into a slinky black dress and a pair of fancy heels.

Her polished appearance contrasted sharply with the project site where four of Ben's guys were tearing out the kitchen of a suburban Cape Cod and preparing to install a new one. Solid honey oak cabinetry, hardwood floors, dark granite counters—the finished product would be a showplace featuring the custom high-end finishings he wanted Hawk Construction to be known for.

"I'm sorry—Hadley, was it?"

"Halie," she corrected. "As in Sex Goddess, Inc. CEO."

He was probably supposed to be impressed. "Why are you telling me?"

He understood Reese needed to go through the motions of the Slut Hotness program for her job, but he'd be damned if he was going to be a *part* of some makeover program that made her feel like she needed to dress in revealing clothes and sleep around. The program may be hotter than the latest iPhone, but Reese didn't need it.

Halie narrowed her eyes and studied him. Feeling less like a stud in a work belt and more like a bug under a magnifying glass, Ben resisted the urge to squirm.

"Tricia tells me that you're Reese's best friend," she said.

"Sure." He shoved his hands into his pockets and rocked back on his heels. That label, *best friend*, pissed him off a little this morning. Sure, he cared about Reese, spent time with her, would do most anything for her. But he was also a man, and he was getting a little irritated with Reese forgetting that.

"She'll need your help to get through the program," Halie said. "As I was saying, it's more difficult than people anticipate. I really push my clients outside of their comfort zones."

His phone buzzed and a glance at the screen told him one of his subcontractors was on the line. So as not to appear rude, he sent the call to voicemail. He really needed to get back to work if he was going to keep this job on schedule. "What do you want me to do?"

"When will you see her again?"

He lifted a shoulder. "We usually meet at Luke's place for drinks on Thursdays."

"That will be perfect." She pulled an envelope from her purse and handed it to him. "Give her this when you see her."

He took it and raised a brow. *This* was what she'd interrupted him at work for? He turned the envelope over in his hand. "Listen, I appreciate you giving Reese a job, but I don't want anything to do with this."

Halie set her jaw. "Be honest. Reese is more than a friend to you."

Ben flinched. "Excuse me?"

"It's in your eyes when you talk about her." She smiled. "It's nothing to be ashamed of. You want her. Stop fighting it."

"You're mistaken."

"Do you really think she's on the path that is best for Reese?" Halie asked. He was about to suggest that Halie didn't know shit about Reese and should quit making assumptions when Halie said, "She's entering into a vulnerable time, a sexual awakening. Do you really want to see her fall into an affair with the wrong man?"

Hand extended to return her letter, he froze. Coffee churned in his stomach at the words—his deepest worry uttered aloud. He studied Halie and tucked the envelope into his pocket.

Halie was studying the house. "You're renovating that place?"

"Yeah. We're gutting it, giving it an open floor plan, a custom kitchen, and some gorgeous built-ins." It was a small place, but it was the caliber of job he wanted Hawk Construction to be known for.

"Ever do anything bigger?"

"In my former life." He grinned. "I used to manage a crew for Whittingman Homes. I wanted the experience before I took Hawk Construction over from my father."

Halie whistled. "Fancy. But has this company ever handled something bigger?"

Not even close. "What do you have in mind?"

"Ever hear of McCormack Manor? Just outside the city?"

Hell, who hadn't? "Sure. That yours?"

"My grandpa left it to me when he passed, and I'm thinking of remodeling and moving in there after my fiancé and I marry. We're interviewing contractors now. Maybe I'll have you take a look." Her eyes looked far away when she spoke of it—not the hard-edged man-eater she came off as when she talked about her program.

"I'd love to." He did his best to keep his cool as he handed her a business card. This was exactly the opportunity his company needed.

"I'll be in touch," Halie said, turning toward her car.

"I'll give her your letter," he called after her. "I'll help her if I can, but I'm not going to seduce my best friend just so she can complete your program."

Halie turned and raised a brow. "Who said anything about seducing her, Mr. Hawk?"

***

"Reese! It's so good to have you in the office!"

Reese looked up from a pile of HR forms to find her new boss wrapping her in a hug. "Thank you," she said. "I'm glad to be here." Glad and feeling a little guilty about all the benefits that came with working for Halie's successful empire.

Halie looked around the office. "It's not huge, but I hope this space has everything you need."

"It does," Reese said. This was the first time in her life that she'd had her own office, and she even had a window. "Hopefully I'll be done with this paperwork by lunch and I can get started on our New Year's Eve event."

"Oh, about that." Halie lowered herself into a chair on the other side of Reese's desk and crossed her long legs. "I'd like something sooner. Let's do a Halloween masquerade ball and something else for New Year's. Don't you think that would be fun?"

Fun? Sure. *Impossible* would also be an appropriate word choice. "Yeah, I can see why that would be fun, but we have to find a venue, find a caterer, market the event. Maybe next year—"

Halie pushed up from the chair. "No, this year. I need to see you work your magic."

"By having so little lead time, we're—"

"You can do it, Reese. Stop underestimating yourself." She headed toward the door, then stopped. "Oh, and I want to start a Sex Goddess for seniors program, so start looking into some promotional opportunities for that as well. We'll meet tomorrow and discuss your ideas."

Reese could only stare at Halie's back as the woman swept out of the room. Suddenly, she felt no guilt about the perks that came with being an SGI employee. She was going to earn every penny.

CHAPTER SIX

"What are you writing?"

Reese slammed her notebook closed and bit her lip. The PitStop was picking up with the Thirsty Thursday crowd and Reese had been so engrossed in her SG 101 homework she hadn't even noticed.

Ben looked down at her, his green eyes crinkled with concern. The man was masculinity personified with his thick five o'clock shadow and steel-toed boots.

Been there, rejected by that, she reminded herself.

He cocked his head to the side. "What's different? Did you cut your hair?"

Her hand instinctively went to her hair. The no-ponytail rule seemed simple on Sunday, but the reality of her wavy hair in Chicago humidity made her wish Halie had cited more exceptions.

"It looks nice." He reached for her notebook again, his work-roughened fingers brushing the backs of her hands. "Come on, what's in the book?"

"Nothing, just..." *Just writing down miscellaneous sexual fantasies.*

At the beginning of the week, Reese had sent Halie an email with her description of Reese the Sex Goddess. She'd made it as far-fetched as possible so Halie would let her move to the next step. The sooner she could get through this, the better. Two minutes after she'd clicked send, Halie had burst into her office.

"You're good with words." She'd rubbed her hands together, eyes bright. "I think this is going to be key for you. I'd like you to keep a notebook and write down any and all stray fantasies you have."

Reese should have known better than to laugh. Halie hadn't scolded her but had said, "I can't name names, but this worked for a former client—a certain actress who may or may not be known for her excellent lips and her many adopted children. I didn't think she'd make it through the program. So insecure. So unaware of her sexual power. This exercise…well, most women fantasize more than they realize. Writing it down makes you slow down and enjoy it. It's a perfect step two for you."

So, Reese had started creating lame little fantasies and jotting them down in hopes of convincing Halie that she was the kind of woman who saw a copy machine and imagined a hot office romp and not an efficient way to duplicate expense reports.

She was totally faking it. But who knew faking it could be so much fun?

Her last entry had been a rather elaborate fantasy about Mark Hawk and some creative use of his soundboard. And if she'd made herself write it only after having a graphic fantasy about the *other* brother? Well, there was no harm in correcting an errant thought. What counted was that she was correcting the thoughts to begin with. She wasn't going to be the girl mooning over her best friend like she had been in those days before Lance.

Ben arched a brow. "What's in there?"

"Forget it." She bit her lip. "Sit down. I need to tell you something."

He pulled out a chair. "Sounds serious," he said, taking a seat.

"It kind of is."

"More slut fantasies?"

"Sort of."

He reached across the table again. She smacked his hand before he reached her book. "What the heck?"

"This is my private journal," she said, clutching it to her chest.

Ben rolled his eyes. "Damn, what are you writing in there? Dirty stories?"

"What if I am?"

"Then I want to read them."

She groaned.

Ben grinned.

"Do you remember what Lance said about our relationship?"

Ben's smile fell away. "You're not getting back together with him, are you?"

She shuddered. "No. Of course not."

"Okay. Then *why* are we talking about him?"

She bit her lip. "Listen, I know he was a jerk, but he wasn't an idiot."

"We're all entitled to our opinion," Ben grumbled.

"He said the way you flirt with me was what kept him from asking me out for so long. He thought I was…yours."

"In that case, I'm sorry I didn't flirt with you more."

Dropping her gaze to her beer, she took a breath. "He said our body language is inappropriate. It gives people the impression we're a couple."

Lance hadn't been so kind. He'd told Reese that Ben was having his cake and eating it too. Ben kept Reese to himself while dating whatever women he wanted.

Across from her, Ben leaned back in his seat. The casual observer might think he was relaxed, but Reese could see the tension in his jaw. "He was jealous."

Reese shrugged. "Probably. I thought that was all there was to it, but lately…" Lately, she'd found herself falling into the same patterns she'd been stuck in all those years she'd been waiting for Ben, and Sex Goddess Boot Camp had made her realize it. "Lately, I've thought maybe Lance had a point."

"And what's that?"

"We spend too much time together. We need to cool it a little. Be more like normal friends." She flinched even as she said the words. They hurt to say, but she needed to do what was best for them both.

"Normal friends?"

"How many dates have you had since I broke up with Lance?"

He crossed his arms. "Enough."

"You know you've dated less since I've been single, and that's my fault. I needed a friend, and you were there. I was grateful for that—I *am* grateful." She shook her head and laughed. "It sounds like I'm dumping you."

He studied her for five hard pumps of her heart. "Aren't you?"

"No, not at all. It's just…we've been down this road before, and we know how it ends."

The side of his mouth drew up in a lopsided grin. "Are you worried you're going to fall in love with me, Reese?"

She snorted and the tension between them fell away. "Hardly."

"Let me help you through Sex Goddess 101." The words seemed to shock him as much as they shocked her.

"You'd just love that, wouldn't you? How do you figure you'd help?"

Ben propped his chin on his fist and wriggled his eyebrows. "With some inspiration for dirty stories?"

"You wish." She studied him. "Maybe you can help."

"Now we're talking. I'll call the guys and see when they can install a pole in the basement."

"A pole?"

"For dancing lessons."

She scowled. "You know what, if I need any help, I'll just call your brother."

Ben growled and narrowed his eyes. "Okay, so what kind of

help do *you* have in mind?"

She shrugged. "The women you date are…" The ceiling didn't offer up the words to make this conversation any less awkward so she shifted her gaze to him. "You know."

He raised a brow. "Profoundly lucky? Eminently satisfied?"

Reese rolled her eyes. "I was going for *sexy*. Or…confident. I don't know. They have that *thing*."

"Thing?"

"That sexy thing that makes men drool."

"You've lost me."

"If I'm going to get through this program, I need to be more like the women you date."

He straightened. "Wait. You're serious?"

She frowned. Had it really come to this? Letting Ben Hawk, of all people, help her become sexy? Her lovesick college self was somewhere inside her, whimpering. "Yes. I think so."

He reached back and pulled an envelope from his pocket and handed it to her. "Halie visited me at work on Monday and told me to give you this."

Reese scowled. "Why didn't you give it to me sooner?"

"I was too busy trying to figure out which of my exes you want to be like." He leaned back in his chair and tapped his fingers on the table. "The poet who said I was the inspiration for her best work?"

"Hardly."

"The lingerie model who wanted me to have a threesome with her sister?"

"She wasn't a lingerie model, she was a woman who didn't understand the difference between under- and outer-garments,"

"How about the kindergarten teacher who liked it when I took my feet and—"

"Stop!" She shuddered. She knew more than she ever wanted to about that particular woman's fetishes. Really, it was best to just change the subject.

She pulled the paper from the envelope, unfolded it, and groaned as she read step three.

"What is it?"

She tucked it into her back pocket. "Nothing that can't wait."

"Are you still breaking up with me?"

She sighed. "I wasn't dumping you. I was saying we should put some distance between us. Date more. Make our interactions more *appropriate*."

"Same thing."

"You can't seriously want to help me with this program."

"Let me prove I'm not the evil influence Lance made you believe I am. Let me prove you can have a healthy dating life without changing our friendship."

"And you're going to do that by helping to turn me into a Sex Goddess?"

"Why not?"

***

Tall, blonde, and stacked, the woman strode into Mark Hawk's office like she was ready to give orders. The look in her eyes said she'd knock over anyone who wasn't interested in taking them.

A smile curved Mark's lips. He wouldn't mind taking orders from this tall drink of water.

"Can I help you?" he asked, tossing aside a memo to stand and offer a hand.

Ignoring his hand, she pushed her oversized sunglasses onto her head and studied him. "You're the man they call The Hawk?"

"The one and only."

"I'm Halie McCormick, Sex Goddess, Inc."

This morning just got better and better. "Pleasure to meet you. I've heard a lot about your work." He grinned. "I approve."

Miss Sex Goddess, Inc. narrowed her eyes. "And what do you think you know about my work, Mr. Hawk?"

Nothing about this woman said "naïve," so Mark imagined

she was well aware that, on air, he referred to her Sex Goddess Boot Camp as "Slut Camp." Nothing about this woman said "laid back" either, so he also imagined she didn't appreciate the nickname, even if he did say it with utmost respect.

"I know I like the results," he said.

He got a smile for that.

He liked her smile. It took some of the hard lines from her face, made her look softer for a moment. When the smile fell away, she was all business and hard angles again.

"To what do I owe the pleasure?" he asked.

Halie smoothed the back of her skirt and took a seat across from him. She met his gaze before she spoke. "You're a man who appreciates beautiful women. Is my assessment correct?"

Mark shifted in his chair, feeling a bit like an animal being backed into a corner. "It's not a secret."

Halie gave a sharp nod. "And what makes a woman beautiful? What makes her sexy?"

If he were on his show, he'd say "big tits and a tight ass." Hell, maybe he'd say that if he was out with the guys, but he knew as well as any other hot-blooded male that a woman needed neither to be sexy as hell. "Confidence," he answered, meaning it.

Another sharp nod. "I'm in the confidence business. I instill it in my clients."

"You make them believe they're sexy, and then they are." It was brilliant, really.

She didn't answer, only pulled a picture from her purse. "You used to work with Reese," she said, handing it to him.

In the picture, Reese looked like her typical self. Self-conscious smile, oversized clothes, diminutive posture. Damn, she was cute. Nothing like the women he dated. Everything like the women he preferred. He was so damn sick of living a fake life. "Yes."

"She's recently enrolled in my program."

Mark raised a brow. "No kidding?" For some reason, he instantly thought of his brother. What did Ben think of Reese being a pupil of the famed Sex Goddess, Inc.?

"I want you to ask her out."

Mark's head shot up, but Halie didn't look like she was joking. "Excuse me?"

"Reese. I want you to flirt with her, woo her, and ask her out. I want you to play a part in her transformation."

"Yeah, I don't think—"

She put her hand up, stopping him. "She's not sexy, right?"

That wasn't the problem. Not by a long shot. Mark's eyes dropped to the picture, thinking of the way Reese blushed when he walked into a room, the way she averted her eyes, as if just looking at him was a carnal act. She hadn't always looked at him like that, but ever since her boyfriend had moved out, the way Reese looked at him made him feel like a Greek god.

And ever since her boyfriend moved out, Ben had been looking at Reese like she was a goddess.

It was all a fucking mess that made him feel guilty. About the secrets he kept from his brother. About the reason she looked at Mark like that. About the past.

"I'm not looking for a relationship," he told Halie.

Halie laughed, surprising him. "Neither is Reese."

Hell. Maybe that was why she was suddenly so infatuated with him. Because back when she'd been looking for love, she hadn't wanted anything to do with Mark. It was nothing new. He understood what women expected from him. Why should Reese be any different? "Why do you want to involve me in this?"

A slow, devious smile curled her lips. This woman was dangerous. "Think about what could come of it. Use your imagination."

He didn't have to. He could easily list ten reasons why he'd like a woman like Reese on the other side of a candlelit table. And one why he couldn't. "She's Ben's."

Halie arched one perfect brow. "Is she? He's interested? Romantically? He's told you this?"

Fuck. No and no.

"More importantly," Halie went on, "does Reese want him?"

"Well, once—"

"I'm not talking about the past. Does she want him *now*?"

"I hadn't thought of it like that," Mark muttered. He shouldn't want anything do with Reese, but that hadn't stopped him six years ago and it didn't stop him now. "Listen, I appreciate what you do, but I think you'll need to find someone else for this. It's too complicated."

Halie stood, smoothing her skirt again. She withdrew a business card from her purse. "Think about it."

And he did, but not for the reasons she thought.

CHAPTER SEVEN

"What's sexier than a Halloween masquerade ball?"

"Exactly," Reese said, clutching the phone and breathing a giant sigh of relief. In a week's time, she'd found a location, a caterer, and a band, and now she'd secured a sponsor in Corrella's Closet, a high-end lingerie store. "Would you be interesting in donating an item or two to our silent auction as well?"

"Oh, I have just the thing," Corrella purred. "I'm so excited I can be part of this event. I adore Halie so much. Her program saved my marriage."

Reese's phone buzzed, and she grabbed it as the woman detailed the troubles in her pre-SG 101 marriage.

Her phone said she had a text from Ben, so she slid her finger across the screen to open it.

Brunch at my mom's in the morning? Or would that send your potential dates the wrong message?

Reese bit back a smile.

"But suddenly," Corrella was saying, "all these men from my past were showing up in my life and I took a closer look at *my part* in ending all those relationships. It was eye-opening."

"That's wonderful," Reese said as another text message made her phone vibrate in her hand.

If it would help, I'll be rude to you the whole time. Call you names, flip you the bird. Whatever Lance would have considered appropriate between friends.

Reese stifled a giggle and forced her attention back to her phone call. "I can't tell you how excited I am for you to be a part of our event. Almost Home makes a difference in so many women's lives."

"Happy to do it, Reese," Corrella said. "Send that contract over, and I'll get to it first thing Monday."

Reese ended the call and turned her attention back to her cell.

Can you give me a ride? she typed.

Pick you up at nine.

She imagined this was what it was like to have an addiction. On the one hand, she knew she needed to change things between her and Ben if she really wanted to eventually have a meaningful relationship. On the other hand, he was her best friend, and being around him—whether people wanted to call it flirting or not—made her smile.

Reese had met Ben in college, but not in the typical way college friends meet. They hadn't met in their dorm or shared a beer at a party. Instead, Ben had been privy to one of Reese's most embarrassing moments.

The blind date had been Masey's idea. She knew a guy who had a brother who sounded *perfect* for Reese. Reese hadn't been so sure but Masey had talked her into it through a series of clichés. *"It'll be great!" "You're only young once!" "You need to let your hair down and have some fun!"*

Reluctantly, Reese had agreed. It wasn't as if she wanted to be single, but bookish and a little awkward, she didn't have a great track record for attracting guys.

They'd decided to meet at a bar by campus. She'd be the brunette in the red shirt, he'd be the guy in the Yankees cap.

After walking in the bar doors a few minutes early, she took a seat at the bar. She wore a pair of Tricia's jeans. When Reese objected they were too tight, Masey had insisted they highlighted her curves. And as she sat at the bar, they squeezed her thighs and she felt suffocated and hot even though she had paired them with a light knit red tee.

At Masey's urging, she'd left her hair down, and the heat in the bar had her sweating under her heavy hair. Sweat accumulated at the base of her neck. Twisting her hair, she held it off her neck.

"Hot day out there," the bartender had said.

Reese looked away from the door and looked up. "What?" Tall, broad shouldered, sandy blond hair, and kind green eyes, the sight of him had her darting her tongue out to wet her lips.

He smiled and grabbed a glass. "Looks like you could use a drink."

"Would you hate me if I wanted to start with water?"

"Not at all," he said, filling the glass with ice.

When she accepted the water, she was all too aware of their fingers brushing. She took a long drink before she spoke. "I thought I'd be escaping the summer heat when I decided to stay in Chicago for the summer."

He waved a hand. "It'll pass." The pub was deserted, and he propped his elbows on the bar and leaned toward her. "Where you from?"

"Kentucky," she said.

"And you came up here for school?"

"University of Chicago," she supplied. "But no redneck jokes, okay?"

"What? Couldn't get into Yale?"

She rolled her eyes.

"You're a junior?" The door chimed as he asked, and he waved to the patron.

"Yes, I—"

"Are you Reese Regan?" someone asked behind her.

Reese's breath caught and she hopped off the bar stool. She'd nearly forgotten why she was here.

"Hi!" She offered her hand, taking in the man before her.

Really, it seemed unfair to judge his appearance after talking to the hottie behind the bar. Her date was cute. Average height, slim build. A few scraggly pieces of dark hair stuck out from under his ball cap.

"You must be Trevor," she said.

Trevor looked her over, his gaze sliding slowly from her carefully tamed hair down to her cute but sensible ballet flats.

Reese wasn't the kind of woman who got a lot of once-overs, and if this was how they felt, she hoped she never would be. Trevor's gaze wasn't so much appreciating as it was appraising, and everything about his body language said he wasn't impressed.

"Damn," he muttered, finally bringing his eyes back to her face. "I told Derrick no fatties."

Then, as if that settled everything, the asshole turned on his heel and walked out of the bar.

Reese swallowed hard against the bile rising in her throat. Cheeks burning, she turned to retrieve her purse and run back to her summer sublet.

The bartender stopped her with a hand over hers. "If you leave now, you'll just feel like shit for the rest of the day."

She squeezed her eyes shut, unable to look him in the eye after he'd been witness to her humiliation. "I can't imagine staying is going to change that," she said softly.

Slowly, she opened her eyes and stared at the floor. The warmth of the bartender's hand left hers but she still couldn't look at him.

She took a deep, fortifying breath. *Time to put your chin up and go home.*

"Hey." He ducked to catch her eye. The bartender stood on her side of the bar now. "Don't you dare," he said softly, "give that loser one more thought."

She looked into his eyes, swallowed hard. "Okay."

He gave a curt nod. "That-a-girl." Stepping back, he winked. "Now tell me what your drink is. It's on the house."

"I don't suppose you any good wine," she hedged.

He slid around the back side of the bar and chuckled. "This establishment caters to the college crowd, so unless you idea of a *good wine* is cheap white zin—"

Reese shuddered. As an impoverished college student, she

couldn't really afford the good stuff, but her parents had brought her up on fine wine. "I'll pass, thanks."

"This is what you need," he said. He poured her a shot of amber liquid and pushed it across the bar.

Reese frowned. "What is it?"

"Tequila. Drink of choice for any self-respecting heartbroken college girl."

She scowled. "I am not heartbroken. I'm mortified."

"You're thinking about the ass again." He nudged the shot an inch closer. "This will correct that."

She gave a sharp nod. "Fair enough." She threw it back and winced as it went down. It hit her belly hot and fast, making her draw in a sharp breath. "Well, then."

He refilled her glass.

She shook her head and held up a hand. "I know my limits."

He raised a brow. "Have you stopped believing what the asshole said yet?"

Point taken, she threw back the second shot.

When he smiled at her, the warmth in her belly grew beyond the boundaries of the hot trail left by the tequila. "I'm Reese," she said softly. "Thanks for saving the day."

"Ben." He whisked the empty shot glass and wiped the bar in front of her. "And I didn't do a damn thing."

Something pulled inside her chest as she studied him. She swallowed. "So, what about you? Are you a student?"

"I'm finishing up a degree in construction management—two semesters left."

"Oh, so you're my age."

He chuckled. "Not unless you, Miss University of Chicago, are also on the six-year plan."

She waved a hand. "Doesn't really matter in the end. What are you going to do with that degree?"

"I'm going to build houses for people who have more money than they know what to do with." He leaned forward on his elbows. "What about you?"

Reese reached for her water. "I'm in public relations.

Actually, I stayed in town this summer because I was taking an internship, but it fell through. This morning." She forced a smile. "It's turning out to be a gem of a day."

Ben frowned and snapped his towel toward her. "Hey, what about that charming bartender you met today? That part wasn't so bad."

Reese bit her lip, her cheeks warming. He was *flirting* with her. "I think he was trying to get me drunk," she said, voice low. "But he is pretty charming."

Ben propped himself on his elbows and leaned forward. "And handsome?"

"Don't push your luck," she said. Her cheeks were full-out burning now.

"You're cute when you're embarrassed."

His gaze dropped to her lips and Reese stopped breathing. His Adam's apple rose and fell as he swallowed. God, he was sexy, and man alive did she want him to kiss her.

She parted her lips, leaned forward a fraction of an inch. Movements so small someone across the bar probably wouldn't have seen them, but they both knew it was an invitation.

Ben snapped upright and made work of straightening some bottles.

Reese inhaled deeply, looking for sanity in the deep breath. He'd seen her be embarrassed and he was trying to be nice. She wasn't the type of girl to pick up a hunky bartender. Men like him—tall, charming, handsome, a body like oh-my-God—didn't date women like her—short, frumpy, awkward, a body like oh-my-Jenny-Craig.

She pulled a few bills from her purse and threw them on the bar. "I should be going," she said with as much cheer as she could muster. She slid off the barstool.

"Don't go."

She stopped and turned to see him standing, thumbs in pockets, a sheepish grin on his face.

He gave a half-hearted shrug. "I'd feel better if you'd let me escort you home. You know, after pushing the hard stuff on you and all."

She shook her head. "It's okay. I walked."

He stepped forward, pressing his palms against the bar. "Still." He spotted her money and shook his head, holding it up for her. "What's this?"

"For my drinks."

"No way. Those were on me." He left his post and tucked the bills into her purse. "My relief will be here any minute. Let me walk you home. What do you say?"

"You really don't—"

The bell over the door rang as a tall, lanky man strolled in.

"Speak of the devil," Ben said. He shoved a hand in his pocket and came up with a set of keys that he tossed at the other man.

He snatched them out of the air. "Your house on fire, Hawk?"

"Reese, meet Luke. Luke, meet Reese."

Luke raised a brow. "Nice to meet you, Reese." He and Ben exchanged a look Reese couldn't quite interpret.

"You too," Reese said.

"I'm going to escort my friend here home," Ben said, shocking Reese by sliding an arm around her shoulders. "She's had a crappy day."

Luke set his jaw. "Just be careful, Reese. Sometimes we do things when we're feeling down that we wouldn't have done if we'd given it some thought."

Reese watched the looks the friends were exchanging. There was something going on here. Was this guy trying to warn her about Ben? Did she need to worry about walking down a busy street in the middle of the day with this guy she didn't know?

"Have a nice shift," Ben said, leading Reese toward the doors.

"Bye, Luke," Reese called over her shoulder.

Once they were outside, Ben dropped his arm. "Where to?"

Reese shook her head. "You want to tell me what that was about?" she asked, gesturing toward the bar.

"I don't know what you mean," he said, but his eyes said he knew very well.

Reese propped her hands on her hips. "I've had a crappy day, Ben. I'm not interested in being a pawn in some game between you and your friend."

Ben grimaced. "Shit," he muttered. "Listen, I'm sorry if I made you feel like that. I really just want to make sure you get safely to wherever you're going."

Reese nodded slowly. She started walking, knowing he'd follow. "Guys are never this nice to me," she confessed. "Unless you count my dad." She meant the last as a joke, but it came out sounding as pathetic as she felt.

"Do you ever give them a chance to be?"

She turned. "What's that supposed to mean?"

They came to a crosswalk and stopped while they waited for a break in traffic.

Ben raised a shoulder. "Guys aren't invincible. We're afraid of being rejected too. Maybe you are so convinced all guys are jerks like the one you met today that you shut them down before they have a chance."

They crossed the road and Reese thought about it. Or tried to. More than anything she was trying to figure out if Ben was interested in her or if he just had a really bad case of Nice Guy Syndrome.

"My apartment is right up here," she said, turning onto a side street.

They walked in silence. When they reached the front doors of her building, Reese studied her feet for a minute, wondering what to do next. She wanted to see this guy again, but despite all his kindness today, she had no idea how to make that happen.

"Listen," he said softly, "I could probably get you hooked up with a summer internship in PR."

She snapped her head up and studied him. "Really?"

His gaze was all over her face. Was he trying to size her up for the position or memorize her? "Give me your number and I'll see what I can do. I'll call you tomorrow."

"Oh. Wow." She reached in her purse, searching for a pen. "Let me—"

He handed her his cell. "Why don't you put it right into my phone? That way I don't lose it."

She keyed in her name and number, trying not to let her nerves show. "I don't even know how to thank you," she said, handing back the phone.

His fingers stilled over hers. "How about we say you owe me one?"

Her stomach knotted with anticipation. "Fair enough."

He treated her to that wickedly adorable grin.

She took a breath, steeling herself for uncharacteristic bravery. "I don't mean to, you know."

"Mean to what?"

If she was going to do this, she needed to go all in. "I don't mean to shut guys down. So...if you're afraid of being rejected..." God, could she be more awkward? "Do you want to come up? Keep redeeming my day?"

Ben's face fell. "I'm sorry. I can't." He backed away, as he'd suddenly discovered she had a deadly contagious disease and he was afraid he might not escape her. "I'm sorry, Reese. I just...can't."

CHAPTER EIGHT

"Reese!" Caroline Hawk exclaimed the moment Reese entered her kitchen. "Come here and give me a hug!"

Reese warmed as the woman hurried toward her, mop of gray curls bouncing. When she reached Reese, she wrapped her in a tight hug. "Thank you for inviting me," she said, squeezing the woman in return. "I don't remember the last time I had a home-cooked breakfast."

She pulled away and narrowed her eyes at Ben. "Why didn't you bring her sooner?"

Ben sighed and lifted his palms. "I thought maybe she had something better to do with her Saturday mornings than raise her cholesterol count?"

Caroline swatted him. She shifted her gaze to Reese and gave her a once-over. "Skin and bones, this one. Needs a good meal." Then, on a mission, she waddled back to the kitchen.

Reese followed Caroline and the smell of coffee and bacon.

"It's our lucky day. Your brother is joining us this morning," Caroline said as she stirred the contents of a simmering pan.

Ben stilled. "You don't say."

She nodded, wafting the steam toward her nose. "Yep, he's making the time. You know he's normally busy with production meetings and whatnot."

"Bullshit," Ben muttered.

Reese nudged him and narrowed her eyes.

Ben lifted a shoulder, unapologetic.

"He's real excited to be seeing you guys. Told me Reese is leaving him at the station for some big promotions director position. Doesn't get to see her much anymore."

Ben stomped to the coffee pot and poured himself a cup.

"Ben!" his mother scolded. "Where are your manners? Our guest might like a beverage as well."

Ben poured a cup of black coffee and handed it to Reese.

"Thanks," she said softly.

"You might ask her what she wants, you putz," Caroline said.

"I *know* what she wants," he grumbled.

Reese hid her grin in her mug. The coffee was hot and rich. She had no idea how, but this woman made the world's best coffee. "He does," she said, sighing with pleasure. "Your coffee doesn't need anything but a cup, Caroline."

"You flatter me," she said, turning back to her stove. "You two relax. The food will be ready in a minute."

"Let me help you, Ma," Ben said, and so began the requisite argument over whether or not the woman would allow her son to work when he was her guest.

The scene was familiar to Reese and made her heart ache a little. She'd come to a lot of Hawk family brunches when she was finishing her undergrad and the months after. They had been her surrogate family when the distance between herself and her home in Kentucky had seemed too far.

As always, Caroline finally acquiesced and allowed Reese and Ben to carry a few items to the table. They were all filling their plates with scrambled eggs, bacon, and biscuits and gravy when Mark strolled in.

"It smells delicious in here, Ma," Mark said.

Caroline popped up from her seat to hug him, then pulled out a chair. "So glad you could finally find some time to visit your lonely mother." She heaped food onto his plate.

"Aw, Ma," Mark said, "I thought you'd need extra time for Dad now that he's retired."

She waved a hand and slid the plate in front of him before lowering into her own seat. "Save your excuses for those pretty girls you date and never call back."

Ben choked on his coffee, and Reese bit her lip.

"Caroline, I've missed you," Reese said.

Mark winked at Reese across the table. "You see how gorgeous Reese looks with her hair down, Ma?"

Caroline glowered. "She was gorgeous with it up. What's wrong with you? You think women need to dress and primp just to please you."

Mark sighed and lifted a hand in frustration. "I'm trying to say something nice about our guest and you turn it into an insult. Now you made her feel bad and made me look like an ass."

"You are an ass," Ben muttered.

"Don't talk that way to your brother," their mother warned.

Reese grinned into her coffee.

"Tell me about the company, Ben," his mother prompted. "How's business? Are you keeping busy?"

"I'm trying to land a renovation that could net us more profit than all of last year," he said. "Actually, it's for McCormack Manor. Reese's new boss owns it. It was her grandfather's home, and she wants it fixed up to live in after she gets married."

"That's lovely," Caroline said, pressing her hand to her chest.

"McCormack Manor? Really?" Mark asked, looking impressed.

"I didn't know that," Reese said.

"Gorgeous place." Ben took a sip of juice. "I talked to some other contractors who have been out there. Word is, the place has good bones but nothing had been updated since the eighties. I'm hoping Reese can put in a good word for me so they'll give me a chance to bid the job."

Reese put her fork down and turned to him. "You know

I'm happy to talk to Halie about it. Why didn't you say anything?"

Ben lifted a shoulder. "I hadn't gotten around to it."

"You shouldn't have to grovel to get a job," a scratchy voice said from the hallway.

Reese didn't miss the tick in Ben's jaw as his father came to the table.

"I'm not groveling, Dad. It's called using my connections."

"Same thing. And this is what you're trying to turn my business into." He shook his head as he settled into a seat. "Kissing a bunch of rich ass."

"No cursing at my table," Caroline snapped.

"If Mark was running the company—"

Mark blanched. "Dad—"

"Well, he's not." Ben put his napkin on his plate. "I'm sorry you had to settle for your younger son, Dad, but me using connections to get business is no different than when you got jobs because your pals recommended you. The only difference is these jobs are bigger and the clients have money to pay the bill."

"The difference is you think you're better than the company your father gave you."

Reese dropped her gaze to her lap.

"I'm trying to *save* the company you gave me. There's a reason Mark was so eager to let me run what could have been his." Ben pushed back from the table. "Excuse me, Ma. I'm not hungry."

***

Ben squeezed the porch rail at the squeak of the front door. He didn't want to talk to his family right now. Not to his mother or brother, who always failed to stand up for Ben, and not to his father, who never failed to be disappointed, no matter how hard Ben tried to make him proud.

After college, Ben had decided to prove himself by working for one of Chicago's top builders. Between his experience, his degree, and his drive, he'd been a hit. He'd moved up quickly in the company, and after two years he was managing jobs bigger than Hawk Construction had ever seen. But it hadn't meant a damn thing to his father.

Soft fingers kneaded the tight muscles at the base of his neck and pulled him from his thoughts. He relaxed his shoulders. *Reese.* "I'm sorry about all that."

"Why didn't you tell me?"

He turned and pulled her against his chest. She had no idea how good it felt to have her here—in his arms and standing by him when his family wouldn't. "You haven't exactly been making yourself available to me lately."

"I know. I've been…busy. I'm sorry."

She had been busy, but she'd also been avoiding him. When he thought about their little talk on Thursday night, he wanted to pull her into his arms and never let her go. She'd been trying to ditch him. When he'd realized it, the terror had gripped him so tightly, he'd said the first thing he could think of to make her change her mind. And now what? He was going to help her dress like a slut and pickup guys in bars?

"You know I would have made time if you needed to talk." She squeezed him tighter.

He breathed in her scent, brought his hands up to tangle in her hair. "I like your hair down."

She pulled back and dramatically tossed it over her shoulder. "Yeah? Does it say *Sex Goddess*?"

Something thick and tight knotted in his chest. "Something like that."

"Well, this is just the beginning. Tomorrow is the big makeover day. For all I know I'll come out of it a platinum blonde with a boob job."

He winced. "You don't need the job *that* badly."

"I thought guys liked blondes." She wrinkled her nose. "Don't think I can pull it off?"

The tightness rose to his throat and he didn't trust himself to answer. "You want to get out of here?"

She nodded, heading toward the car. No insistence he work

things out with his dad, no suggestion that their leaving might be misinterpreted. She just walked to the car.

They were on the interstate before she spoke. "Do you mind if we swing by the mall?"

"You hate the mall."

"Yes, I do. Which is why you're coming with me." She cast a sideways glance at him. "Anyway, I need your help."

"Why? Need to pick out some new lingerie for your Slut Hotness lessons?"

Her cheeks blossomed red.

He grunted. "You're kidding, right?"

Reese folded her arms and leaned back in the seat, avoiding his eyes. "Unfortunately, I'm serious. Halie wants me to throw away all of my underwear, and I figure I better have my new undergarments before my shopping trip and makeover tomorrow."

He bit his lip against a laugh. "Have a nice collection of granny panties?"

She turned to him, eyes narrow. "No. They were those cute cotton boy short panties. You know what I'm talking about? Tell me, what's so wrong with those?"

The grin dropped from Ben's face. He knew exactly what she was talking about, and there was nothing wrong with those. Not a damn thing.

He had first-hand experience with just how sexy they looked on Reese. It had been a trip to a country winery with friends, they—the two single people—had been put in a room together, and since Reese didn't seem to register he was *male*, she hadn't even bothered to find the bathroom before changing into her pajamas. She'd just quietly gone to the corner and stripped down to her undies before pulling on a pair of flannel pants.

He choked back a groan at the memory. "So, why do you need me?"

"Halie gave me a horrifying chunk of cash and explicit instructions on what to do with it. I'm supposed to wear sexy underwear at all times." She sighed. "And it's come to my attention that I'm not so good at identifying what's sexy and what isn't."

Or Madame Sex Goddess isn't, Ben thought. Yeah, Halie was clueless. There was nothing wrong with panties that showcased a woman's ass like those did. But apparently she wanted something different. Something more overtly sexy.

He pulled onto the exit ramp and changed lanes, heading downtown. Swallowing hard, he asked, "Are you asking me to help you pick out underwear, Reese?"

"No," she said.

Ben exhaled, his shoulders dropping. His threshold for that kind of torture wasn't—

"I'm asking you to help me pick out panties, bras, and nighties."

He groaned audibly and hit his turn signal. "In return, you'll model them for me, right?"

She smacked his arm. "No."

"That's just not fair," he said. "What's in it for me?"

"You're the one who talked me into doing this, Benjamin Hawk."

"I told you to fake it," he said.

"Well, I'd rather not have to *fake* having enough panties to get through the week, so this is happening. Anyway, you told me you wanted to help me through the program."

"I was thinking less *shopping buddy* and more *strip tease instructor.*"

***

Ben was taking this mission very seriously. She'd suggested the mall and he'd vetoed the idea and driven to Corrella's Closet. The high-end boutique was known for its sexy designs and rich fabrics, and once they were in the store Ben surprised her by being perfectly comfortable surrounded by women's lingerie. He flirted with the staff and handled the garments with confident care.

"This stuff is so expensive," she hissed. It wasn't news to

her. She'd contacted Corrella's about being a sponsor for the ball precisely because of how expensive her wares were. Somehow the prices meant something different when she imagined spending it on herself.

"Good thing you're not paying, then."

She peeked at another price tag and gaped. "Wouldn't it be better to use the money to—I don't know—feed a small country?"

"Black," he said, handing her a black lace underwire bra.

It was gorgeous. She imagined he was used to seeing beautiful bras like this on the women he dated. She frowned. "It's not practical. I couldn't wear it under most of my clothes."

He grunted. "It's perfect." He looked at her, and her face must have given her away because he sighed. "Come here," he said softly, taking her by the wrist and directing her toward a full-length mirror in the back of the store.

He stood behind her, both of them facing the mirror, and held the bra up in front of her. "Picture this," he said softly, his breath brushing her ear, "with that dark hair of yours falling around your shoulders."

He trailed off. In the mirror, their gazes met. A rush of something unexpected shot through Reese and tension pulled between them. The decision to ask him had been impulsive and spurred more by guilt about her recent avoidance than by good sense, but here she was, bonding with her best friend over sexy lingerie.

"Beautiful," he said softly.

"You two are just too cute!" the sales clerk screeched, breaking the tension. "Molly," she said over her shoulder to the other clerk, "don't you just love it when couples shop together? I love it. It's so sweet. Don't you love it? Have you found everything you're looking for? Is this for an anniversary? A special night?"

Reese, snapped from her daze, turned to the woman. "Oh, we're not—"

"Not celebrating anything in particular," Ben said, turning

and putting his arm around Reese's shoulders. He grinned. "I just wanted to do something special for my wife here."

Reese forced a smile but nudged Ben in the ribs. "My *husband* really enjoys this kind of thing," she said. "You know, fashion, beauty tips, shoes. He's one of those…" She wrinkled her nose as if trying to find the word. "Metrosexuals?"

But that didn't shake him. He just winked at her and…pinched her ass.

"Ben!"

He grinned. "What, *sweetie*?"

She narrowed her eyes. "You are bad."

His lip twitched. "Do you think my wife and I could get a dressing room?" he asked the sales clerk without taking his eyes off Reese's face.

"Ben, they don't allow people to be in their dressing rooms together—"

"It's okay," the clerk said, chuckling. "Our rooms are private." She summoned them with a wave of her hand before disappearing into a small doorway at the back of the store.

"Come on, *baby*," he said.

Reese's cheeks burned as she followed Ben to the dressing rooms.

"Here you go," the clerk said, opening a door. "Anything else I can get you?"

Ben nodded and passed the lace bra he'd been holding to the saleswoman. "I'd like one of these in red and pink and the matching panties."

"Thong or bikini cut?" the clerk asked him.

Reese propped her hands on her hips. She was *right here*.

"Oh, she definitely needs both."

"Wise man."

"We'll also want to try those sheer white nighties and the black and pink lacy corset thing on display at the front."

Reese's eyes widened. "Ben," she hissed.

"The merry widow?" the peppy attendant said. "Absolutely."

Reese closed her eyes and groaned. When she opened

them, Ben had settled into a chair in the dressing room, leafing through a magazine like it was his flipping home away from home. "What are you doing?"

"Helping," he said without looking up at her.

"Ben," she hissed.

His lip twitched but he didn't look up at her.

"You're punishing me for making you do this, aren't you?"

"Why don't you tell me your little secret and I'll go easy on you."

Reese stilled, swallowed. "What secret?"

"The reason Halie thinks you need her program?"

Her shoulders relaxed and she let out her breath. "Not gonna happen."

Miss Peppy returned with an armful of lace, satin, and chiffon, saving her from further interrogation.

"I grabbed a couple other items I thought you might like too," Miss Peppy said.

"Put them over there," Reese said, pointing to the changing room across the narrow hallway. "You know, so the reveal is more dramatic," she lied.

"Killjoy," Ben called after her as she pulled the door closed.

In the dressing room, Reese froze. That was one big pile of sexy, and she felt like it was sizing her up. She narrowed in on the merry widow. Might as well put that one in the discard pile from the start. She couldn't imagine she'd ever wear—

"Start with the merry widow," Ben called.

The way he said it made her pulse kick up. Okay, so it was sexy. Ridiculously sexy. Meet your man at the door and never make it past the foyer sexy. And she was a little curious—

"If you plan on making your way to the essentials, you better get moving because panties will be the last items we pick out."

She bit her lip and pulled off her clothes, shimmying into the merry widow. Her eyes widened when she turned to the mirror. Okay, so…yeah. Definitely hot.

The piece accentuated her narrow waist, and it must have had magical powers because it lifted her small breasts in a way that created cleavage, and made her too-wide hips look like something that belonged in a centerfold, not on a treadmill.

Suddenly, she was struck with the ridiculous desire to open the door and show herself to Ben. To let him see the piece he picked out. On her.

Her mouth went dry as she imagined his response, his eyes running over her.

Seek opportunities to give and receive pleasure.

Well, why the heck not? He'd seen her in less.

She opened the big wooden door.

"So?" she asked.

Ben's head snapped up from the magazine and his eyes went wide before he moved them down the length of her body and slowly back up. "That one," he said softly. "I don't give a damn what else you get, but you're getting that one."

A smile tugged a Reese's lips, a rush of pride and pleasure—and something else she'd rather not examine—rushing through her.

She slipped back into the dressing room, pulling the door shut behind her.

She leaned her head against the wall and took in a shaky breath.

"Hey, Reese," Ben called through the door.

She peeked her head out. "Yeah?"

"Either your phone is trying to let you know you have a message or you left your vibrator in your purse again."

She coughed. "It's probably just Halie. I sent her a text earlier to tell her step three was in progress."

Ben frowned. "What was step three?"

"Underwear shopping," she mumbled.

Ben grunted. "I see. You really are just using me to get through your program."

"Do you mind?"

"Hell no."

CHAPTER NINE

Halie had told Reese to bring a friend. She'd said she'd send a driver. She *hadn't* said the driver would be in a limousine or that they would spend their day being served and pampered like royalty.

"Thanks for coming with me," Reese said when they were settled into chairs for hair and makeup. They'd already had massages, facials, and pedicures, and after hair and makeup they'd move on to shopping.

"Are you kidding me?" Masey said. "I should be thanking *you*. This is amazing."

Resisting the urge to squeal, Reese grinned. "I know, right?"

"Tell me how the program's been so far." Masey sipped at her glass of champagne as someone worked on her highlights.

Reese frowned at her reflection. The stylist was combing some color into her hair—*"for dimension"*—and wrapping it in foils. Reese looked like she was trying to protect her brain in case of alien invasion. "There hasn't been much to it," she admitted. "Actually, I'm really surprised how easy it's been."

Masey grinned and leaned back in her chair. "Well, maybe you're a natural."

Reese snorted. "Hardly. I have a feeling we're just warming

up." She dropped her gaze to her champagne flute and the bubbles gathered against the curve of the glass.

"Okay, if things are going so well, why do you look so glum?"

"I told Ben we needed space, that I thought we spent too much time together, that we're too familiar for friends." She frowned. It sounded ridiculous, even more so when Masey remained silent. "Physically, you know? I'm going to start dating, and we have to think about the impression we give people."

"People, like Mark?"

Reese shrugged. "Maybe."

Masey swallowed audibly. "What did Ben say?"

"He said I was dumping him and he wouldn't let me. He said he'd help me get through SG 101 and prove we could be friends and date other people."

"He wouldn't *let* you?"

Reese nodded. "Then yesterday I went lingerie shopping with him. At Corrella's."

Masey raised a brow.

Reese looked at her hands. "And I might have modeled a particularly sexy merry widow for him."

"But it was completely platonic, right?"

Reese lifted her head to see Masey's skepticism written all over her face. "I know. It's ridiculous, but I think he might be the best person to help me through the program."

"Really?"

"I'm comfortable with Ben." She bit her lip. "It's not like we're making out or anything."

"Uh-huh."

"As long as we're honest about what we want and don't want, who are we hurting, right?"

Masey nodded slowly, her expression blank. "Have you convinced yourself yet?"

***

When Reese walked into the PitStop Sunday night, she didn't just turn heads, she broke necks, and Ben wanted to break something on every man looking in her direction.

Unfortunately, his brother and Luke would have to be first in line.

She was hardly in the door before Mark sauntered toward her, taking her hand and running his gaze over her like he was inspecting a new car. "Christ almighty, look at you."

"Reese, is that you?" Behind the bar, Luke let out a low, smooth whistle.

Ben's gut knotted. She looked gorgeous and put-together and sexy. Her chin was up and her eyes were bright. Her hair floated in soft waves around her face, drawing attention to her full lips and big brown eyes. And her outfit? Just unfair. A fitted skirt hugged her excellent ass and was topped with a shirt she'd left unbuttoned past her collarbone. Ben's fingers itched to finish the job.

He wanted to tell her to go back to how she'd been before. And at the same time, he wanted to press her up against the nearest wall and show her just how *inappropriate* he could be.

Reese's cheeks blazed, but she looked Mark in the eye as she said, "I clean up pretty decent, huh?"

She only revealed her discomfort in the way she cut her eyes to Ben, and he doubted anyone else noticed. He was the safe one, he realized. She was uncomfortable with the attention and she knew Ben was safe. Did she know he had a dick?

Mark looked her over—head to toes and back. "That Sex Goddess woman works wonders."

Wrapping an arm around Reese, Ben pressed a kiss to the top of her head. At Luke's cough and the quirk of Mark's lips, Ben realized he'd unconsciously delivered a message to every man in the bar: *Mine.*

Reese sank her teeth into her bottom lip. "You like it?"

Ben's heart pumped harder, faster at the way she looked at him—as if his answer was the only one that counted. Oh, yeah, she was perfectly aware he was a man.

Her big brown eyes were lined, making them look bigger

than ever. Her lips looked plumper than usual, covered with some sort of shiny stuff he wanted to lick off. "Yeah." The word came out gruffer than he'd intended.

She smiled—really smiled—for the first time since she'd walked through the door. "Really? You don't think I look like a fraud? Or like I'm trying too hard?"

He stepped back so he could see her. Now it was his turn to run his eyes over her, to take her in one delicious curve at a time. With a resigned sigh, he shook his head. "Sorry."

She frowned. "Sorry?" She propped her hands on her hips. "It can't be that bad."

He held up his palms. "Sorry. I'd tell you what I think but you'd find it inappropriate and tell me you can't be my friend anymore."

She smacked him in the stomach with the back of her hand.

Side-stepping another swat, Ben shrugged. "I'm trying to save our friendship."

"You're so bad."

If being bad made her smile like that, he didn't intend to be good anytime soon.

Luke passed a beer to her over the bar, and she said, "Tell me what you think. Seriously."

Ben let his gaze drop to her mouth and waited a heartbeat. "I'll do you one better," he said softly so no one else would hear. "Meet me in Luke's stockroom and I'll *show* you."

"Okay," she said, looking at her beer. "Point taken."

***

"Look at you!" Halie crooned when Reese walked into the office on Monday morning. She clapped her hands. "You're gorgeous!"

Reese looked down at her fitted skirt and heels and couldn't help but agree. Her makeover had been an amazing experience. She'd expected it to leave her feeling inadequate, but instead she finally felt good in her own skin—perhaps because her skin had been massaged, exfoliated, emulsified, and moisturized.

After they left the spa, they'd gone shopping. Halie's "style expert" had given her a chance to pick out her own clothes, but it became quickly evident that Reese was a lost cause. She always avoided fitted clothes because she thought they were only for svelte women, but Halie's stylist had shown her how much better the right fit flattered her curves.

"Thank you," Reese said. She knew she was standing taller this morning—and it wasn't just the heels. "I know you've spent a lot of money on me and I'd like to pay you back. I don't have it all now, but—"

"Stop right there," Halie said, holding up a hand. "First, I won't hear of it. I lost the two most important men in my life, and it sucked, but now I have more money than God. I console myself by using that money in ways that make me happy—that means treating women like you. Second, the fact that you want to pay me back shows you're coming around." She shrugged as if she was picking up the tab for drinks and not a whole new top-of-the-line wardrobe. "That's payment enough."

The phone on Reese's desk buzzed. She flashed Halie an apologetic smile. "I'm sorry. We should talk more later, but I need to get that. I have half a dozen phone calls I'm expecting this morning."

As she backed out of the room, Halie called, "Don't apologize. That's why I hired you."

Reese snatched up the phone. "Reese Regan, SGI."

"SGI? Is that what you're calling yourselves now?" The crackly voice bespoke a woman with a sixty-year-old pack-a-day habit. "What? Ashamed to use the real name?"

"Mrs. Wisenowitz," Reese said into her receiver, "so good to hear from you." Mrs. Wisenowitz was the director of a senior center near Ben's parents. The woman had no filter and an opinion about everything.

"You always say that, but if you miss me so damn much, you should come visit. You know where I work."

"You're right, Mrs. W. I should visit more often, but I'm not calling about me. I'm calling because my boss wants to start a Sex Goddess for seniors class and I wanted your thoughts on it."

"I'm not so old that I don't have any tricks up my sleeve, Miss Regan. Sex Goddess classes for seniors," she huffed. "Like we don't know how to shake it."

Reese bit her lip. The woman had to be creeping near ninety. "Call me Reese, Mrs. Wisenowitz."

"Bah! I'd like to call you Mrs. Rich Man, but I can't do that now, can I? When are you going to find yourself a man and settle down?"

"Oh, don't worry. I will someday. I just haven't found my Prince Charming yet."

"You don't need Prince Charming, you need Prince Wealthy, I'm telling you!"

Reese laughed but didn't dare comment. Mrs. Wisenowitz was a wealthy widow who would go on and on about how she married Mr. Wisenowitz for his money but would bite off the head of the first person who dared to suggest the same thing.

"Well, think about it, and let me know if you'll be joining us for our masquerade ball." Pulling up her seating chart, she studied the VIP seats. She wanted every one of those top-dollar seats to be full. "You could bring a date."

"You know what my problem is, Miss Regan?"

Reese bit her tongue before saying, "I can't imagine."

"The men my age don't interest me."

"Well, why not?"

"They're *old*!" she cracked.

Reese laughed. "Well, we'll be doing a bachelor and bachelorette auction, so you could always pick your date up once you arrive."

"That's the best idea I've heard since my beautician said I wasn't too young to be a platinum blonde. Is that beau of yours going to be up for auction?"

"I'm not with Lance anymore, Mrs. W."

"I'm not talking about that idiot. I'm talking about that boy you spend so much time with—Caroline's boy. He's no bum, that one. Real hard worker, good family too."

"Ben? Ben and I are just friends, and no I don't think he's going to participate in the auction." But it couldn't hurt to *ask*, and Reese added a note to her list.

"Want to keep him for yourself, huh?"

Reese shook her head. "There will be plenty of handsome bachelors for you to bid on."

Reese just needed to find them.

CHAPTER TEN

Reese needed male escorts, and she knew just where to find them.

"Hey, beautiful," Luke called as she walked in the door. "What's the special occasion? I haven't seen you two nights in a row since you took that job."

"It's been busy, but it will slow down after the masquerade ball." She hoped that, but was beginning to get the impression that all of Halie's staff—Halie included—worked long hours and wouldn't have it any other way.

"Ben's in the back on a business call."

She crossed her arms. She was friends with all of them, so why did Luke assume she was here for Ben?

"Beer?" Luke grabbed a pint glass from a wall and filled it without waiting for a response.

"Oh, thanks," she said as she took the beer. "Hey, can I ask you something?"

Wiping his hands on a towel, he turned to give her his full attention. "Sure. What's up?"

"You know me and Ben really well. Do you think he and I give people the impression that we're dating?"

"Or that you wish you were?" a deep voice said behind her.

Reese turned to see Mark Hawk.

"Hey, kiddo," he said, running his gaze over her. "I like the way you wear those jeans."

She'd changed into a new pair before leaving the office, but she'd left on her strappy black heels, bright pink dress shirt, and dangly silver earrings. Her cheeks warmed but she made herself say, "Thanks." Then, "People think Ben and I want to be dating?"

Mark shrugged. "Don't shoot the messenger."

Reese shook her head. "We don't. Want to date, I mean. It's not like that."

Luke grunted and Mark said, "Good to know."

"What's good to know?"

Reese jumped at the sound of Ben's voice.

"Reese was telling me how much she likes her new job," Mark said, winking at Reese.

She shot him a grateful look. "I do. It's nice being challenged. Actually..." She rolled her shoulders back and pasted on her best smile. "I was hoping you three might consider helping me out by volunteering for my bachelor and bachelorette auction."

Ben and Luke groaned, but Mark said, "Whatever you need."

Reese crossed her arms and looked at Ben and Luke. "Are you going to let him show you up like that?"

"Yes," they chorused.

"Well, think about it at least."

"You staying for a beer?" Ben asked, waving toward his table at the back of the room.

"Sure," Reese said. She looked to Mark and Luke. "You guys joining us?"

Luke shook his head. "Sorry, I'm doing inventory while I have Mark here to watch the front."

"Next time," Reese said, but Ben was already pulling her toward the back, a grin nearly splitting his face.

"I owe you one," he said as they settled at the table.

"One what?"

"A favor. When you got here, I was on the phone with

Halie. She was calling to set up a meeting to discuss my quote."

"I didn't do anything but tell her the truth. She'd be lucky to have you."

Her phone buzzed, interrupting her.

"Mind if I check that?" She pulled her phone from her purse, but one look at the screen had her groaning.

Step Five: Ben tells me you're at the bar. You're a young, modern woman. Don't wait for a guy to pick you up, pick one up yourself. End your night with a kiss and Sleeping Beauty may fully awaken.

"What?" Ben asked.

"It's Halie with my next step."

"What's next?" Ben grabbed her phone.

"Don't!"

But it was too late. He was scowling at the screen. "What she doesn't know won't hurt her."

"What do you mean by that?"

"I mean fake it, just like we planned. Tell her you did it."

"You mean *lie.*"

He handed back her phone. "Is there a difference?"

"You don't have to look so unconvinced. I can pick up a guy as well as the next girl." She frowned. "I just need someone to tell me *how.*"

Toby Keith crooned from the jukebox.

"Try standing on the table and asking for a volunteer."

Reese snorted. On Mondays Luke's wasn't exactly at maximum capacity. Those who were here, lingering over their dinners and watching football, were like Ben, blue-collar guys in work boots and ball caps who weren't too politically correct to whistle at a beautiful woman or listen to Mark Hawk's radio show. Reese could just imagine their reaction if she did what Ben suggested.

"You're not seriously considering—" His grin vanished. "Reese?"

She met his eyes. He lifted her chin with one finger, and the intensity in his gaze sent a lick of pleasure up her spine.

This was Ben. Her friend. *Friend. Buddy. Pal,* she reminded her girlie parts. Apparently, Sex Goddess 101 gave those parts a mind of their own. "Yeah?"

He swallowed. Time tripped on repeat as their gazes tangled.

No. This was Ben. Ben was...Ben. They were friends. They laughed and joked. There was no *tangling* of gazes. Sure, he'd made sexually suggestive comments to her before. He was a guy. *Once* she'd made the mistake of thinking there was more between them.

It was an embarrassment she didn't intend to repeat.

But this was different. She could have sworn his eyes dropped to her mouth for the briefest moment before he pulled his hand away. "I'm beginning to hate this program."

Reese released her breath. "Why?"

"First of all, you don't need it."

Well, that was...sweet. A big fat lie, but sweet.

"You still want my help?"

She crossed her arms. "How do you intend to help me with *this*? Aside from your brilliant standing-on-tables advice."

He lifted a shoulder. "What? You're not afraid to show me your moves, are you?"

She straightened and smirked. "You forget I'm a slut in training."

"Prove it."

Crap. He just called my bluff.

Ben pushed away from the table and winked at Reese as he backed away.

At the pool table, he racked a set of balls.

She was toast. Broad shoulders, narrow hips, beautiful green eyes, and a killer smile. Ben didn't fade out next to his brother, who was taller, darker, broader, and louder. He should have, but he never did.

The only thing Mark had going for him that Ben didn't was that Mark had never broken her heart.

She exhaled sharply, pushing away the thought, and headed for the bar. If ever a situation called for liquid courage, this was it. Had she *ever* made out with a random guy? Despite all her bluster, even if Ben could show her how to pick one up, she wasn't sure she was the kind of girl who could stick her tongue down the throat of a perfect stranger.

Mark had moved behind the bar and was pouring a middle-aged man a drink. She waved to him.

"I'm going to need something stronger," she said.

Mark raised a brow. "Really?" He looked at his watch. "Isn't it Monday?"

Reese glanced over her shoulder to the table where Ben was lining up a shot. As if he sensed her looking, Ben lifted his attention from the line-up to her and mouthed, "Chicken?"

"Tequila," she said, turning back to Mark. "Make it a double."

Mark shook his head but poured the amber liquid in the glass.

She shot it back before she could over think it and winced as the liquid burned down her throat. "Wow."

Mark chuckled. "Rough day?"

Reese looked at Ben again. He'd pushed his sleeves up, exposing toned forearms. God bless manual labor. That man had really nice forearms.

And this wasn't the first time she'd noticed. Not even the first time this week.

Damn. No wonder people got the wrong idea about them.

"Things are about to get interesting," she said, shifting her gaze back to Ben, who winked at her as he made another shot. "Another?"

Mark coughed. "Reese, I don't think—"

She turned to him and set her jaw. "How many times have I seen you serve pretty girls far past their tolerance?"

"None of them were as pretty as you."

"Liar."

He put a hand to his chest. "You wound me."

She tapped her glass, waiting.

He shook his head. "Fine. But, hey, don't complain to me when you want to die in the morning."

She smiled at him as he poured another shot. Why was she thinking about Ben when she could be thinking about Mark?

Dark, messy curls, those intense dark eyes. She watched him as she sipped the shot.

"Just promise me you won't drive home," he said.

A slow smile curled her lips as a plan hatched. "You offering to give me a ride?"

He leaned forward on the bar. "Any time, and you know it."

"I'm not sure I do know," she said softly. Her mind spun and landed on her memories of the summer she'd met the Hawk brothers. The best and worst summer of her life.

"Reese, I've only kept my distance because you asked me to."

"We both know I'm not your type, Mark."

He lifted a brow. "What do you know about my type?" His voice was soft and it catapulted her back in time. The sun pouring in the window and the hot body next to her, her head pounding from too much tequila the night before, the panic that set in the moment she realized what she'd done.

"You never told him," she said.

His dark eyes looked sad as he exhaled heavily. "I promised I wouldn't."

"I just might take you up on that ride," she said. "I'm supposed to kiss someone tonight…step five." She lifted her glass and he snagged it away from her. "Hey!"

"If I get to kiss you again, I'm going to make sure you remember it this time."

She glanced over her shoulder and caught Ben watching them. She was warm and climbing up a buzz, but that didn't change the fact that Ben was her best friend and deserved fair warning if she was going to mess around with his brother. She couldn't take another secret.

She pulled her wallet from her purse and Mark waved it away. "It's on me."

She shook her head. "Let me pay."

He inched a little closer. "Let me take you out."

What was she waiting for? "Okay."

Mark grinned. "Really?"

She shrugged. "Why not?"

"I'm gonna hold you to that."

Did she need to explain that she wasn't interested in anything serious? He was Mark Hawk. He was king of "not serious," right? "I'll be right back, okay?"

"Sounds good," he said.

She strode across the bar and gripped Ben's arm. He didn't need to teach her how to pick up a guy. She'd already done it. "Hey."

He dropped his gaze to where her fingers curled around his wrist. "Hey, yourself."

The jukebox clicked to an old Nine Inch Nails grind, and Reese's hips started to sway to the beat. Good old tequila made any beat a dancing one.

Ben was looking at her funny.

"What?" Reese smiled, feeling light and carefree. "Come on." She headed back to the alley so they could talk in private. He followed wordlessly.

When the door slammed shut behind them, she leaned her head against the brick of the building and closed her eyes, enjoying the contrast of her heated skin in the cool evening air. When she opened her eyes, Ben was studying her, that funny look still creasing the corners of his eyes.

"I've got it figured out," she said. She was almost giddy with the thought of a date. It would be fun. It'd been so long since she'd just had *fun* with a guy. And she could do this. It really didn't have to be complicated at all. Six years ago, when she'd woken up in Mark's bed, she'd still been hung up on Ben, but things were different now.

Tomorrow she'd report to Halie and move on to step six. Heck, she was halfway there.

"You do?" Ben asked. His pulse thrummed at his neck.

Impulsive with tequila, Reese reached up and touched the pulsing skin. "Your heart's pounding."

"Yeah." His gaze dropped to her mouth.

She cocked her head. "I'm going to let Mark take me out."

His jaw ticked. "Don't be stupid, Reese."

"Wha—"

He cut her off with his mouth. He cupped her face in his big palm and brushed his lips across hers. He was warm and gentle.

And from the first brush of his lips, she wanted more.

Maybe tomorrow she'd blame the tequila or maybe she'd blame the lingerie shopping or the dirty stories she'd been logging into her notebook. Maybe she'd blame their tragic beginnings and her endless months of waiting for him to want her, but right now she didn't even need an excuse. She moaned against him, loving the feel of his mouth, the light scratch of his scruff. Ben was so painfully male. A hot and delicious, long-denied craving.

Ben slanted his mouth over hers and slipped his tongue inside. He tasted like beer. Like male. Like something wicked and addictive. He wasn't one of those rushed and sloppy kissers. He kissed like it was making love. Like he had all the time in the world. Like his most important task was kissing her. It was a kiss she'd known once and had never forgotten.

He slid his hands under her jaw and into her hair.

Reese grabbed a fistful of his shirt in her hand and pulled him closer, thinking of his eyes on her in the dressing room, thinking of the only other night they'd kissed.

He slid a hand behind her ass and lifted her, pressing her between the wall and his body and nestling his hard-on right between her legs. She gave a moan of approval and rubbed her tongue against his, exploring his mouth for all she was worth. She reached around his neck and slipped her fingers into his hair, tugging gently. Groaning, he pressed himself even closer to her. She cursed the day denim was invented. She wanted *closer, closer* even as part of her brain told her this was a mistake, told her to end this before they ruined everything.

He tore his mouth from hers and latched onto her neck. Sucking, nibbling, tasting until her eyes closed and she arched into him.

His teeth grazed the shell of her ear. His breath was hot as he whispered, "I'll be damned if I'm going to let *my brother* help you with the best parts of this program."

Reese froze. "Ben." She pushed at his chest and he backed away, lowering her softly to the ground.

Keeping a hand behind her head, he toyed with her hair.

Reese studied him. His face was serious, his eyes hot, pupils dilated when she asked, "What was that?"

"A kiss." The corner of his mouth twitched. "A fucking good one."

Her jaw worked, but none of the words that came to mind would do. "This is my fault. The lingerie shopping—"

"Was the best part of my weekend." His mouth tipped up in a lopsided grin. "And I think you liked it too."

God, had she. "We're playing with fire."

"We're adults. We can manage a little fire."

Her gaze dropped to his mouth before she forced her eyes away. *Been there. Rejected by that.*

She swallowed and forced a smile. "Thanks. On to step six, right?"

He brushed a thumb over her lip. "Let me drive you home?"

Her mind was spinning—from the kiss, from the tequila, from the hard-edged craving pumping through her veins—and she knew she couldn't drive herself. Mark had offered, but then she'd kissed Ben, and—*Oh, hell.* "Sure."

Reese was vaguely aware of Mark watching them as they returned to the bar to retrieve her purse. She was vaguely aware of his eyes on them as they left together. But mostly she focused on putting one foot in front of the other and not making a big deal of the first kiss she'd shared with Ben since the day they met.

On the ride home, she did her best not to think about how pathetic she'd been in those early days of her *friendship* with Ben, those days when she was so sure he would come to his senses and she waited like a loyal dog.

She thought she'd wised up since then, thought she'd accepted that she and Ben were a much better friend match than romantic one. And yet, one kiss later and she was twenty-one again and hopelessly crushing on the sweet guy who said all the right things, touched her in all the right ways, and wanted nothing she had to offer.

CHAPTER ELEVEN

The day Reese had met Ben, she hadn't expected to see him again—ever. She'd done a fantastic job scaring off the sweet guy who'd shown a little interest in her. And yet he'd shown up at her door at ten o'clock at night, staring at her mouth like he'd like to lick it.

"It's late," he'd said softly. "I don't know what I'm doing here."

"Ben—right?" As if she could have forgotten.

He nodded.

Oh, hell, this guy was a master at sending mixed signals. His body language said he was ready to bolt, but the way he was looking at her mouth was so darn hot. "Did you forget something?"

"Yeah."

She waited several long heartbeats then raised a brow. "What did you forget?"

"This." He slid his hands into her hair and lowered his mouth to hers.

His lips were hot and soft and his thumbs stroked the edge of her jaw as she opened under him. Her hands found his chest and she curled her fingers into his shirt and tugged him closer.

He drew back, and his eyes burned into hers. This was the

way men were supposed to look at women. This was the way she always imagined feeling and never had.

"We wouldn't want you to forget that," she murmured.

"This is crazy." He touched his forehead to hers.

"Yeah," she said, but she tugged his shirt again. "I'd invite you in, but that seems to scare you off."

He groaned and rubbed his thumb over her bottom lip. "I wanted to. I want to now."

His mouth was on hers as she walked backwards into her apartment. She heard the door slam, and slid her hands into his hair. She wasn't the kind of girl to do this. She barely knew this man and she was ready to strip bare for him.

He pushed her against the wall and found the hem of her shirt. She lifted her arms over her head and he pulled it off.

She moaned against his mouth and tugged at his shirt, her hands sliding up and under the soft cotton and connecting with a solid wall of muscle and heat.

He pulled back and let her remove his shirt.

"Wow." Her gaze was glued to his chest. Her jaw was on the floor. "You can't be real."

His lips tilted up in a grin and his eyes swept over her. "Let me prove it."

Her stomach was doing some impressive acrobatics and everything south was nudging her to kiss him again. "I don't even know you."

He rubbed a lock of her hair between his fingers. "True."

"I've never done anything like this before."

"Me either."

Maybe she wouldn't have believed him. Maybe she shouldn't have, but his eyes drifted back up to meet hers and what she saw there was more than sincerity. It was pain and desire and vulnerability all wrapped up together.

Reese kissed him. She pushed herself up on her tiptoes and pressed her mouth to his.

Half a heartbeat later, he had her against the wall. His hot hands tortured her breast through her bra, his mouth doing wicked things to hers.

She wanted so much in that moment. She wanted this man, wanted his hands on her bare skin, wanted his weight on her.

He slid his hand over her bare torso, his calloused hands rough against her bare flesh until he was cupping her through the thin cotton of her yoga pants.

She moaned at the light friction he placed there—wanting this, wanting more.

"You're so damn gorgeous," he whispered against her ear. "I've seen you at the bar before today and have always thought so." He moved his mouth to her neck.

"Why—" She gasped as he found her clit and pressed lightly. She arched to give him better access. God, this man was doing more for her through two layers of fabric than the last man she'd slept with had done skin to skin. "Why didn't you introduce yourself?"

"I was stupid," he said. "But I'm trying to remedy that."

He dropped his head to her breast and sucked hard, drawing her nipple into his mouth through the thin satin of her bra.

"My bedroom—" She was cut off by a ringing phone.

"Sorry," he grumbled. He dug his phone from his jeans and chucked it across the room. The phone silenced. "You were saying?"

"You're crazy." She wasn't complaining. "The bedroom—"

Across the room, the phone clattered against the hardwood floor as it vibrated.

"Voicemail," he explained.

"That's not an angry girlfriend, is it?" She was joking, but he didn't meet her eyes. She shoved him away. "You have a *girlfriend*?"

He stepped back and dragged his hand over his face. "Not exactly."

She thumped his bare chest with the back of her hand. "This isn't a gray area. You either do or you don't." She side-stepped him and wrapped her arms around herself. "That's why you wouldn't come up earlier. That's what your friend was trying to warn me about at the bar."

"Can I explain?"

She snatched his shirt off the floor and shoved it at him. "Go."

Across the room, the phone beeped.

Ben winced. "She cheated on me—"

"So you thought you'd return the favor? Well, I'm flattered, but no thanks."

"It's over between us."

Reese found the couch and propped herself against the backside. "It's over?"

"Yes."

Silenced stretched between them until she said, "Look, there was a reason you walked away when I invited you up earlier. They say the first instinct is the best—"

"Walking away *wasn't* my first instinct," he growled. "But it's fresh, and I didn't want you to be some…rebound thing."

She lifted her head to look at him—dark eyes, bare chest, his shirt balled up in a fist at his side. He was too perfect—the kind of guy she admired from afar. "I don't want to be something you'll regret."

"The only thing I would regret," he said, crossing to her in two long strides, "is leaving here without kissing you again."

"Ben—"

His mouth took hers and she didn't stop him. Didn't want to. She wanted those rough hands on her body, that hot mouth kissing her.

They fumbled their way toward the couch, hands pushing away clothing, mouths seeking out exposed skin.

Reese's leg slammed into something. "Ouch."

"Are you okay?" He dropped to his haunches before her and ran his hands over the backs of her thighs.

"I think the end table attacked me," she whispered.

"I better take a closer look." He stared up at her, eyes hot as he found the waistband of her yoga pants and peeled them from her hips.

Her heart tripped at the sight of him, at the feel of his hands, at the way he watched the path of the dark cotton as he slowly lowered it to the floor.

She stepped out of her pants and stood before him in her blue satin bra and white cotton panties. These weren't undergarments made to seduce a man, but, judging by Ben's eyes alone, she might as well have been in black lace.

His hands returned to the back of her thighs. "Let me look," he said, nudging her to turn around.

She turned and closed her eyes against the sensation of his fingers trailing over the angry spot.

"That's going to bruise," he said softly.

She cast a glance over her shoulder. "It's okay. I'm fine."

"It's a shame to damage such beautiful skin." He put his mouth against her skin, pressing soft kisses and making her forget the pain entirely.

When he opened his mouth and ran tongue and lips up her thigh, she gasped. His fingers traced the edge of her panties along her ass and under to the inside of her thighs and her fingers curled into the back of the couch.

Her panties were damp where his fingers skimmed across them, her legs growing unsteady beneath her.

"Turn around." His voice was deeper, rougher than before.

She turned to face him, looked down to him as he worshipped her body with his eyes.

"You're sure about this?" he asked.

She nodded. "I'm sure."

He positioned her hands behind her back and held both wrists in one hand. He pressed his open mouth between her legs and found her clit through her panties. She whimpered and tried to move, but he tightened his hold on her wrists and moved his mouth against her.

When he pulled away, his chest rose and fell with his breath. He released her wrists but kept one hand in his and led her around to sit on the couch.

She lay down and expected him to follow. *Wanted* him to follow. She wanted his weight on her, his body closer to hers.

He didn't. Instead, he shucked her panties from her hips and sat, one of her legs behind him, one on his lap. His eyes flicked to hers—intense, hot, hungry—before returning to that private space between her legs.

He parted her with his thumb and her back arched as the volatile cocktail of pleasure and anticipation whipped through her.

"Come here," she whispered, reaching out for him.

Eyes flashing to hers, he gave her a lopsided grin. "Not yet." His fingers traced her slick folds and his gaze returned.

He slid a finger into her, out again, slid in a second. She gasped—at his fingers moving inside her, at the look on his face as he watched.

She was no virgin. She'd been with a couple guys, made out with more than that still. Yet, somehow, the way this man *watched* as he moved his fingers inside her was the most erotic experience she'd ever had.

She felt herself edging closer to that elusive summit. Her sex squeezed his fingers, her hips moved—wanting more, more, more.

And when he lowered her head and put his mouth against her clit, she thought she might actually—finally—come.

Her hips lifted off the couch, allowing his fingers to slide deeper. Her breath caught and she grabbed the couch pillow in her fist. Higher and higher, he pulled her.

"Oh, God." Finally. God, she wanted this and she was—

Across the room his phone buzzed and clattered against the hardwood floor, whipping her out of the moment.

Her hips settled back into the couch, and Ben lifted his head, hot eyes finding hers. "Stay with me."

She swallowed hard and squeezed her eyes shut. His fingers pumped in and out of her, and it felt *good*, but the other—that height, that precipice—was gone from her reach.

She couldn't have this man, this sexy man who looked and touched her like she was a sexual goddess, she couldn't have him knowing she was cold, that she froze up with men, that she couldn't experience an orgasm like a normal woman.

He lowered his mouth and took her clit again, and the pleasure was real. It was that reach beyond pleasure that was lost to her. His movements increased in speed and she knew what he wanted, what he expected.

She squeezed the muscles of her sex around his fingers and moved her hips. The phone buzzed and clattered again and she pretended she didn't hear it. She made all the right noises and moved her body in all the right ways. She couldn't let this man know that she wasn't the sexual creature he assumed her to be—so she faked it. And after, when he cupped her gently and lowered himself over her, he was smiling, as if her orgasm had been a gift.

His phone buzzed again.

"Someone's really trying to get ahold of you," Reese said softly.

Ben groaned and pushed himself up. "I'll go turn it off."

He crossed the room and snatched the phone off the floor, but as his fingers moved across the screen, he froze.

Reese sat up. "What's wrong?"

"My ex," Ben said, tucking the phone into his pocket. "I'm sorry about that."

Reese crossed her arms over her chest, feeling exposed. "She's really determined to get a hold of you. Do…do you need to call her?" She'd asked because she hadn't known what else to say.

Ben shoved his hands in his hair and let out a long breath. "No. I've said everything I have to say to her. I don't want her to ruin this."

"How long were you with her?"

His jaw tensed. "Three years."

His phone buzzed again. "I'll turn it off."

She held out her hand. "Give it to me."

Ben handed it over, and she opened the history of texts from "Lisa."

When she read what was there, her heart froze solid in her chest. She forced herself to inhale, and the air burned as she forced it into her lungs. "I'm so sorry." She handed the phone back to him and watched his face go pale as he read the message that had been sent to his phone five times tonight.

This is Lisa's mom. Lisa's been in a terrible car accident and is in ICU at Chicago Methodist. Please come.

She heard his sharp intake of breath and her heart broke for him—this man she'd just met, this stranger who'd been touching her, kissing her, in the most intimate way only moments ago. He sank down into her couch and she knew he'd read the last message.

She's gone.

CHAPTER TWELVE

Ben parked his truck in front of Reese's building and turned off the ignition. She hadn't said a word the whole way home, and it wasn't the good, sexy silence he'd prefer from a woman he'd been feeling up minutes ago. "I'm not sorry I kissed you."

Her knuckles were white where she gripped her purse in her lap. "We're friends."

The words were a punch in the gut. "That hasn't changed," he said softly. "I don't take you for granted."

"We're friends," she repeated.

"Yeah," he growled, "friends who have done a hell of a lot more than kiss."

She froze at that. They didn't talk about that night. Ever. First, because he hated himself too much when he thought about what he'd been doing while Lisa was dying in a hospital room. Later, they were friends and it was easier to pretend that night hadn't happened.

Slowly, she turned to look at him. "We agreed we wouldn't ask each other for more."

Another blow. She was going to hold him to that old promise. He didn't ask why. Not only would his pride not allow it, he knew. He'd fucked up once, and Reese wouldn't give him a chance to hurt her again. He exhaled slowly. "No problem." Hell, he couldn't blame her.

***

"Dad asked me to take some time off work to help with the Granger job."

Ben set his jaw and turned slowly to his brother. Luke's bar was crawling with college kids tonight, making the bar louder and less relaxing than how Ben preferred it. "I've got it under control."

Mark lifted a shoulder. "I have the time coming anyway, and I miss working with my hands. It's no big."

No big. That's how his brother described barging into Ben's worksite and playing boss for a week. *No big.* He gritted his teeth. "It's your company too. Do what you want."

Mark's eyes turned hard and he stared at Ben. "I will."

Luke approached them with a pitcher of beer and a tray of empty pint glasses. "My dish boy wanted to thank you and Reese for the show you put on behind my bar last night."

Ben slid quarters into the pool table and began racking the balls. "There was no show."

"You and Reese?" Mark studied the pool cues on the wall. "What's going on there?"

"Nothing," Ben said. He'd be damned if he was going to talk to *Mark* about it. Hell, he didn't want to talk to anyone about it.

He'd been ready to see if he and Reese could make something more of the chemistry between them. He was sick of sitting on his hands, sick of pretending that their time together wasn't locked and loaded with sexual tension. He'd been ready to try and she'd been itching to end things before they began. Was she still hung up on Mark?

He scowled at his brother. "She said you asked her out."

Luke thumped Mark's chest. "She looks hot now, doesn't she?"

Ben growled and Luke smirked.

Mark lifted a shoulder. "I miss having her at the station."

Bullshit. "Do you even know what she *did* when she worked there?"

Mark leaned over the table and took the first shot, scattering the balls across the green felt. "I'm not as oblivious as you think."

Ben shrugged. "You just suddenly seem a hell of a lot more interested in Reese than you ever were before."

"Do you have a problem with that?"

Fuck yes. "A problem with some asshole who only wants her because she got a makeover? Yeah, I do."

Mark released his cue and it fell on the table with a *thunk*. "Is that what you think of me?"

Ben didn't realize he was closing in on Mark until Luke pushed between them, a palm on each brother's chest.

"Not here," Luke warned, looking to Ben then Mark.

Ben's heart hammered in his ears, and his fists clenched at his sides.

Mark shook off Luke's hand and backed away. "You think you know me, but you're as bad as the assholes who listen to my show."

Ben clenched and unclenched his fists, as if the movement could release his urge to throw punches.

"Who are you mad at here, man?" Luke asked Ben, squeezing his shoulder. "Him or yourself?"

Ben shrugged off his hand. "He's an asshole."

The bell at the front rang and three sets of eyes landed on Reese as she ambled through the door.

The sight of her made all the anger drain out of him. He felt his shoulders relax and watched Mark's do the same.

Jesus. Mark *cared* about Reese. When had that happened? And how had Ben missed it?

Mark pulled his gaze away from Reese and settled it on the pool table.

Ben pressed his cue to Luke's chest. "I'm not up for this tonight." He didn't wait for him to respond before he strode toward Reese.

With every step toward her, he relaxed more. Because she

was here. Because even after he'd kissed her, even after she'd put up that damn wall she was so good at erecting, even after she'd walked away from him, she'd come back.

And now she was smiling at him and he didn't give a damn what his brother wanted.

"I didn't think I'd see you tonight." He trapped his hands in his pockets to keep himself from tucking her hair behind her ear. She looked so soft tonight. Soft and sweet in a little pink-dotted dress that cinched under her breasts and showcased her legs.

"I'm meeting Masey." She wrinkled her nose. "This isn't going to be awkward, is it?"

"No, not at all," he said in a rush. Too much of a rush. He swallowed. "We're still friends. Though I'll be honest—I wish Lance hadn't given you the impression friends shouldn't make out. But I guess I'll be *appropriate*."

She laughed and her shoulders relaxed. "Thanks, Ben."

He watched her walk to a booth in the corner before making his way back to the guys.

Luke and Mark were watching him, but it was Luke who spoke. "So, are you finally going after her or what?"

Ben avoided their eyes as he found his cue stick. "We're just friends." If that's what Reese wanted, that's the way it would be.

At least until he could change her mind.

***

Reese looked up from her computer to see "The Hawk" leaning against her doorjamb. His broad shoulders nearly filled up the small space, his dark, smoky eyes watching her, his hands jammed into the pockets at his denim-clad, narrow hips.

Her fingers paused on her keyboard. He almost looked...vulnerable. She smiled, nearly laughing aloud at the thought. *Vulnerable* was probably the worst word to describe Mark Hawk.

Whatever descriptive word best suited him, the effect was

endearing.

"What are you doing here?"

"I was hoping to talk to you when my guard dog of a brother wasn't around."

She frowned. "Seriously? Why?"

He shrugged and gave a half-smile that, for a moment, reminded her of Ben. "I wondered if you'd forgotten you'd promised me a date. And a kiss."

"Oh." She hadn't forgotten. Not exactly, but she'd managed to finish step five without him, and, mistake or not, she wasn't the kind of girl to make out with two brothers in a single week.

"You're cute when you work," he said, straightening.

Not what she'd expected. Her mouth dried. "Thanks?" The word came out like a question.

He chuckled. "You're not good at taking compliments, are you?"

Reese tucked a lock of hair behind her ear. "It's never been a personal strength of mine."

"I'm surprised. Everyone loves you. You must get compliments all the time."

Her cheeks heated and she grasped for a safe topic. "Have you given any thought to your costume for the bachelor auction?"

His face went blank.

"Do you even read your work emails?"

His lip twitched. "I would if they were ever any *fun*."

She laughed, couldn't help herself. "You're consistent, Hawk. I can say that for you."

"Consistent. Yes, that's how every man dreams a pretty girl will see him."

She shrugged. "There are worse qualities."

Mark moved from the doorway and dropped into one of the chairs facing her desk. "I bet you think my brother is something better than *consistent*."

"Ha! Ben is…" She leaned back in her chair and put both hands in her hair, searching for the word.

"Perfect? Hardworking? All my mother ever wanted in a son?"

Reese frowned. "Wow, there was a lot of resentment there. Where'd that come from?"

Mark gave a bashful grin. "Sorry, old rivalries die hard, I guess."

"I never would have guessed you'd feel so inferior to your brother."

He lifted a shoulder then leaned forward on her desk. "Ben's got it good."

"Sure, but some would argue you do as well."

"He's the Midas of construction. Everything he touches is successful."

"You have a nationally syndicated radio show."

"His profession is universally respected. Something Mom can brag about to her friends."

"You have a great salary. A book deal. Fans across the country."

"Ben has you," he said softly.

Reese flinched then forced a smile. "What do you mean by that? We're just friends." God, she was sick of hearing herself say those words.

He cocked his head. "He's the reason you panicked about what happened between us. Wasn't he? He was a mess about Lisa, but you wanted to be there when he snapped out of it."

She swallowed hard. Mark was too astute. Too on target. "Come on," she said. "We were drunk and frisky and we both know I'm not your type."

"You keep saying that." He skimmed his gaze over her, reminding her that she was closer to Mark's type now than she'd ever been before. "How do you know what my type is?"

A bubble of laughter burst from her lips. "This is so ridiculous."

"What?"

"You're jealous of Ben, Ben's jealous of you. You're both so convinced I want the other and as much as you hate it, neither of you really wants me."

"I wouldn't be so sure." He looked at his hands. "You don't see what you have with my brother transforming into something more?"

Reese swallowed hard. The last two weeks notwithstanding, it had been years since she'd allowed herself to consider having something more with Ben. But just because her libido suddenly had ideas of its own didn't mean it was any better an idea now than it was during her hopeless puppy-dog years.

"I'm not interested in being anything more than Ben's friend."

"That gets me halfway there," he muttered. He gave a half-smile and looked at her through dark lashes. "What about me? Are you interested in being more than my friend?"

She thought of step six, sitting in her phone as the latest text message from Halie. "Mark, I'm not looking for a relationship right now."

"I'm only asking for a date."

"Okay," she said cautiously.

"Next weekend? We start with dinner, maybe head to that drive-in outside of town before it closes up for the season."

Dinner and a drive-in movie with Mark Hawk—a fantasy date. So why did the idea seem no more than a means to an end? Why was she more interested in being able to tell Halie she'd completed step six than she was in the date that would get her there? "It's a deal, then."

His smile turned into a full-fledged grin, changing his face from handsome into drop-dead, take-me-now gorgeous. "Who's the luckiest brother now?"

CHAPTER THIRTEEN

"Do you know how *horny* chinchillas are?"

Ben didn't know, but he had a feeling Whitney was about to tell him. Since listening to a horny chinchilla story beat joining the other wedding guests for the YMCA, he asked, "Seriously?"

"Yes!" Whitney replied, blue eyes widening and a smile spreading across her face. "I mean, I got this thing as a pet for my *daughter*, and every time I turn around, he's sitting in his cage"—she looked over each shoulder and lowered her voice—"*pleasuring* himself. How am I supposed to explain that to my daughter?"

Ben chuckled politely. He really wanted to like Whitney. A tall redhead with big baby blues and a great smile—and an excellent body. She was Ben's type in every way except the one that counted. But when she'd asked him to accompany her to this wedding, he'd broken a cardinal dating rule by saying *yes*. Had he been so desperate for a date?

His phone buzzed, alerting him to a text message. He ignored it.

Whitney smiled. "You are a saint for coming with me tonight." She shook her head as the DJ encouraged everyone to come out to the dance floor for a slow number. "I know

112

this isn't most guys' idea of fun."

Ben shook his glass. "Hey, there's free beer. What guy doesn't like that?"

She grinned. "And that's why I like you." She shot a glance over her shoulder and waved to an elderly couple heading toward the exit.

Lucky schmucks.

"I'll be right back. I'm going to say hi to the Conners."

When she was away from the table, he pulled his phone from his pocket.

Message from Reese Regan.

He tapped the screen to open it, but when he read the message, the smile her name inspired fell from his face.

Long day. Just leaving the office. Heading to your place to use your tub.

The words evoked a vivid image of a sudsy, naked Reese soaking in his master bath. Wet. Naked. His.

He shook his head. Not *his*. Maybe he wanted Reese. Maybe the image of her in his tub had his cock hard faster than a naked woman promising a blow job. Maybe she'd been the exclusive star of his fantasies lately. But she wasn't *his*. She'd made that perfectly clear.

He frowned at his phone then keyed in a response. *You never did tell me what your big secret was.*

What secret?

The one your sister told Halie. The reason Halie was so anxious to make you into one of her slutty converts.

He took a sip of beer and waited for a response. When none came, he typed. *Tell me. A trade for the tub.* He wanted to know. But more than that, he wanted her attention. She'd been avoiding him—canceling morning workouts, turning down invitations to meet him at Luke's bar. She was too busy with work, she said.

It's stupid. Embarrassing.

Try me, he typed.

Was she too busy, or was she avoiding him? And how pathetic was he that he was going to rope her into a texting conversation just because he missed her so damn much?

Just when he thought she wasn't going to reply, his phone buzzed. *I'm bad at sex. A cold fish.*

He caught himself laughing out loud. *Ridiculous.*

Maybe. Still true.

How do you figure? Is this all based on that asshole Lance?

Lance isn't the only guy I've been with.

Right. He knew that. They may have spent six years pretending that night between them never happened, but that didn't mean he'd forgotten it. *Exactly, and I recall your performance as far above average.*

You've idealized it in your memory, then.

Had she just called *him* a bad lover? *Then I demand a rematch. To set the record straight.*

Nice try, but it wouldn't change anything.

I don't believe people can be bad at sex, Reese. People can be bad together—and for the record, we weren't—but not bad at sex. Who told you that?

He glanced up to make sure Whitney was still chatting with the other guests. When she made an apologetic face and held up a finger, he was grateful.

No one told me.

He believed that about as much as he believed Lance wasn't an idiot. *Bullshit. Someone told you or implied it.*

This conversation is not headed where I hoped.

Spit out what you mean and I'll get it back on track.

He watched the clock on his phone and sipped his beer. Three minutes passed before she sent her reply.

I'm saying I've never had an orgasm with a man.

He blinked at his phone but his brain couldn't come up with a response.

I told you that you didn't want to know.

I've heard a lot of women can't during sex, he typed. She had during other stuff. Definitely.

Never.

He looked around. No sign that he was being punked, but he still couldn't be sure. *So you don't count...us?*

There's nothing to count.

The hell there wasn't. He'd been there. He'd heard her, watched her face. *Um…I think your memory is failing you.*

There's nothing wrong with my memory.

Hell, this was embarrassing.

His phone buzzed with a new message from her. *Don't say I didn't warn you.*

He shifted in his seat. *Now I'm going to question every woman I've ever been with. You were very…convincing.*

Thanks, I guess. And think of all the practice I've had since then.

Ben ran his hand down his face. *So…never at all?*

Ha! No, I'm completely capable. Just never with someone else.

Ben let out a long breath. Hell if that didn't feel like a challenge he was itching to take up.

Now you know. I will be stealing a bottle of wine as payment.

A second later his phone buzzed again. *I don't want to interrupt if you hoped to bring your date home. You're sure you're okay with me using your tub?*

Only if you take pictures. A smile tugged at his lips as he keyed the reply.

He watched Whitney hug the old couple as he waited for Reese's next text. Whitney caught his eye and grinned. She'd made it clear that she had a sitter for the night and a room upstairs. It was an invitation he should have been jumping at. Instead he was greedily awaiting another text message.

His phone buzzed.

Don't joke. That's probably one of my ten steps.

As he typed, he knew he wouldn't be spending the night with Whitney, even if it was the smart thing to do. He punched *send* on his message: *Need a photographer?*

***

Reese took a long sip of her wine before sinking deeper into the hot bubble bath. Between shopping, primping, and long days at SGI, all she'd wanted to do was go home and sink into a hot bath. Problem was, her tub was small and about as relaxing as a stone-lined casket. She'd decided without much thought to swing over to Ben's and take advantage of the jetted tub in his master bath. He never used the thing, and she knew he'd be out late at that wedding.

Need a photographer?

He was joking, of course. But his suggestive remarks had started feeling less funny and more serious. And instead of making her laugh they made her...hot.

She hadn't responded. But being in his house after the suggestion—after the kiss, after the tension that was so thick between them she wanted to lap it up like a cat with a bowl of thick cream—suddenly, her mind was spinning with images of Ben, a camera, and her nude body.

The idea of nude pictures would have horrified her just a couple of weeks ago, but now it was an erotic experience she wanted. Ached for.

Had she changed so much in a short time?

And the fact that she wanted *Ben* to be the one behind the camera?

When her cell rang, she snatched it off the side of the tub and answered it without consulting the caller ID.

"Hello?" she said, too lazy with fantasy to open her eyes.

"Is this Goldilocks?" It was Ben's voice, and her body, already primed, grew aroused at the familiar, thick timbre.

"Depends who's asking." A smile curled her lips. She peeled her heavy lids from her eyes to check the bathroom door, but it was still closed.

"This would be the bear whose wine you've been drinking."

"Was yours the wine that was too hot, too cold, or just right?"

His chuckle warmed something in her. "If I were to judge by the half-empty bottle on the counter, I'd say my wine's all right. How's the tub?"

"Glorious." She stretched out again, moaning in pleasure. "Pack your things. Someone needs to live in this house who can appreciate it." She looked at the door again, wondering if he was on the other side. "How was the wedding?"

"Pretty typical."

"Mmm," she said. "Make out with any bridesmaids?"

"Only a few," he said. "Most of the night, I was enjoying the company of a bridesmaid who was detailing the escapades of her pet chinchilla."

"I hear they're horny little creatures." She cared more about his date than she was comfortable with. "Did you bring her home with you?"

"Why would I have done that when I knew Goldilocks was here waiting for me?"

She heard clunking on the other side of the door. Shoes being dropped to the floor. An image of a bare-chested Ben flashed in her mind. It was nearly midnight and he was probably getting ready for bed. The weekend they'd roomed together on that winery tour, he'd slept shirtless in flannel pants. Was that what he wore alone? Maybe he just wore his boxers. Maybe he was the kind of guy who would slide between the covers completely nude.

Water sloshed around her as she sat up. "I'll get out of your hair."

"Relax," he said. "Someone needs to get some use out of that tub."

Her muscles already resembled goo too much for her to protest. "Thanks," she said simply.

"I've been meaning to ask you if you got the next step."

"Yesterday."

"And…?"

And her plans with Mark would take care of it.

"Come on," Ben said. "Tell me."

"You just want to *help* me more."

"Damn right I do."

Her stomach flipped. She wanted everything his words insinuated. "But what if it's not something you'll do?"

"Like what?"

The jets massaged her muscles, working her soreness and her worries away. "Like phone sex."

Ben groaned. "Hmm. I guess I'd be willing to suffer

through that."

"Yeah?" The warmth circling in her belly sank deeper.

"I'm a good friend like that."

"I guess that's lucky for me."

He chuckled. "Ever done it before?"

"No." She closed her eyes, something hot and nervous and needy rushing through her. "Are you out there? Just on the other side of the door in your room?"

"Would it be better if I wasn't?"

She ignored the question, not knowing the answer herself.

"I was at the reception when I got your text." His voice had dropped lower and it came out a little gruff, a little gravelly. "Do you have any idea what it's like to be stuck watching an anniversary dance and get a text from a beautiful woman that she's waiting at your house naked?"

Reese bit her lip. "I didn't say I was naked."

"Aren't you?"

She swallowed as her breathing became shallow. "I am currently dressed in some very fashionable bubbles. Halie would approve."

She was trying to be flip, to make the conversation turn away from the high danger zone where he'd been directing it, but Ben groaned, and this time there was no question in her mind what kind of groan it was.

"I couldn't even enjoy the open bar after that text."

He was putting her on, of course. For the sake of her next step, he was exaggerating the typical reaction any single guy would have to a woman using his tub. But even when she told herself these things, she couldn't ignore the pulling ache between her legs, the wet heat she couldn't credit to the tub.

"You probably say that to all the women who hang out in your bathroom naked."

Maybe it was the wine, or maybe it was the logical culmination of the sexual frustration spinning between them. Whatever the reason, she heard herself ask, "When a girl is in a guy's tub, do you think he thinks about it?"

There was a long silence, filled only by the whirring of the water. "I think about that more than I should. Every time you come over to use it, I wonder if this will be the time you leave the door open."

She sucked in a breath. "It would be easy—too easy—to do." She shifted, letting the tub's swirling water rush between her legs. One hand still held her phone, but the other rested between her breasts, her fingertips tracing an invisible circle.

"Not just easy. Good."

"Someone else could easily fit in this tub with me."

"I might not want to climb in."

"Oh?"

"I might just want to watch, to look at the tops of your breasts above the water, the outline of your body under the bubbles. I might just want to wait until the water cleared enough to reveal your legs…the tops of your thighs."

She let her hand drift lower, tracing invisible circles on her belly now. "That would be better than joining me?"

"It would be torture. But if I was lucky, I might catch you touching yourself."

Her breathing grew ragged and her hand stilled where it was traveling still lower on her abdomen. "That would be good?"

She could make out the faint sound of his choppy breathing. "Hell yes."

She took a breath. "Ben?" His name broke the silence. She wondered if he was in bed, slipped between the sheets. Maybe he was pacing across the soft beige bedroom rug. Or maybe he was standing at the bathroom door, head leaning against the jamb.

"Yeah?"

"You don't have to do this."

"Do what?"

She ran her tongue over her lips, swallowed against the dryness in her mouth. "Phone sex?"

"Is that what you think this is?"

"Isn't it?"

"Nah. It's phone sex when I tell you what I'd do if you

opened that door."

She pressed her head against the back of the tub, closed her eyes against the ache brought by his words.

"Tell me," she said, surprising herself.

He took in a long, ragged breath.

"You've really thought about it?" She skimmed her tongue over her bottom lip, tasted the wine there, wished it was *his* tongue doing the tasting. "Before tonight, I mean. You've thought about coming in the door?"

He could have easily blown off her question, blaming any more-than-friendly thoughts on his male anatomy. Instead, he said, "You have no idea. Every time you bathe here, my bathroom smells like flowers for days."

"Sorry about that."

She heard a brush of fabric and imagined him settling into the bed, imagined his hand settling over his cock.

"You ever touch yourself when you're in my tub, Reese?"

Her breath left her in a rush. She barely gave a thought to denying it. Maybe that would have been the smarter choice, but she wanted this. Wanted this moment, this conversation. Him. "Sometimes."

CHAPTER FOURTEEN

Jesus. Reese touching herself in his tub. He could easily imagine it, had already imagined it a thousand times. "Are you now?"

"I want to." Her voice was soft, quiet without being tentative.

He closed his eyes and pictured her, covered in suds, opening the door for him. Maybe she wouldn't. Maybe she'd stay in the tub and call for him. He wanted that. Wanted her. Wanted to touch her wet body, to wipe the suds off a beaded nipple with his thumb before dipping his hand into the water and cupping her sex, letting his palm rub against her clit as he leaned in to kiss her.

He forced himself to stay seated, propped up in his bed. He eyed the bathroom door. He wanted to pace. Wanted to press his hand against the door as he imagined her on the other side. But he didn't trust himself not to turn the knob. Didn't trust himself not to push the fragile and quickly changing boundaries of their friendship.

He could hear her shallow breathing through the phone, could hear the whirring of the spa jets, the slosh of the water as she shifted.

"Touch yourself for me."

"Ben." Her shaky intake of breath sounded in his ear. "This

is dangerous."

"Maybe." But hell, wasn't it too late? Pandora's box had been opened, and they might as well see what was inside. "Maybe it's not so different than the times you did it before."

She released a strangled laugh. "It's different."

"How so?"

"You're on the phone, for one."

He dropped his hand to his lap and cupped his hand over his cock. "When you did it before, did you ever get yourself off?"

She moaned softly—out of discomfort or pleasure, he wasn't sure. "Yeah."

He leaned his head back and squeezed his eyes shut, imagining her sliding her hand between her legs. "Were you ever thinking of me?"

His heart thudded, filling his ears through the silence that followed the question.

"Yes." A single word, whispered on an exhale, and everything shifted between them. "Do you ever...think of me?"

He squeezed his eyes shut. *Always.* He knew how screwed up that was. He was a guy. His fantasies were supposed to be many and varied. And his were varied all right, but lately they always featured Reese. "Yeah."

The sound she made was half moan, half cry, the sexual frustration thick in the painful note.

"Put your hand between your legs." His voice came out rougher than he'd intended, but at her intake of breath, he knew she didn't mind. "Slide a finger inside yourself for me."

"Are you...God. Ben?"

"I'm here with you. Are you touching yourself?" He knew she was. He heard it in the change in her breathing.

"Yeah." She breathed the word more than said it. "You?"

"Do you want me to?"

"Yes." She sighed into the phone. "Keep talking to me."

He unbuttoned his jeans, freed his cock, and wrapped his hand around it, closed his eyes and imagined it was Reese's hand. "I get so hard thinking about you—naked, in my house, in my tub, steps from my bed."

"I think I always wanted to believe you thought about it. That it turned you on."

He growled and stroked himself. "Touch yourself for me." His voice was hard and rough and he couldn't help it. He was brittle with hard-edged want, with need. He had to hear her come, had to know it was his voice, his words taking her there.

"Ben—God, this is—"

"Amazing? So fucking sexy?"

She hummed in reply. "Are you with me? Are you—" She cut herself off with a moan.

"Am I stroking my cock to the sound of your moans?"

Her breathing hitched. "If you're not, lie to me."

He chuckled, even as his cock pulsed harder, thicker against his palm. "I wouldn't want you to be having a good time all by yourself."

"This is crazy."

He could tell by her voice that she was pulling back, thinking too damn much. "This is nothing. This is a phone call. Crazy is what I want to be doing to you."

"Oh?" She took in another one of those shaky breaths that made him feel like king of the fucking universe. "What do you want to be doing to me?"

Ben opened his eyes and studied the closed door. He let the silence pull tight between them for half a dozen heartbeats before he answered. "I want to lift you out of the water and take you to my bed." He stroked himself, imagining how she'd look, skin warm and pink from the hot water. "I want to feel your breasts in my hands and taste your nipples with my tongue." He squeezed his eyes shut against the sound of her whimper. When he spoke again, his voice was soft. "I want to spread your legs and look at you. I want to taste you—tease your clit with my tongue until you beg for more."

He moved his hand faster, rougher, as she cried out—short little cries and the sound of sloshing water as she rode the pleasure. The sound of her orgasm had the head of his cock swelling. He imagined that it wasn't her hand around him now, but her body, hot and tight and pulsing, pulling his cock deeper. His orgasm came fast and hard, hot liquid hitting his bare stomach.

"Holy crap," she whispered.

He opened his eyes and smiled. He cleaned himself up with the shirt he'd discarded on the floor. "You doing okay in there?"

"You could say that."

He stared at the door between them. "Reese, if you left that door open, I'd be in there in a heartbeat."

"And then what?"

"I think we both know the answer to that question."

"Ben—"

Water sloshed and as the open drain hummed in the background. He could imagine her stepping from the tub, her skin rosy and slick with water.

He was watching the door—waiting for it to open, for her to offer herself to him. The phone beeped to alert him the call had ended. He opened his eyes. She was standing before him in his bathrobe, a fluffy navy blue thing he'd never used and always hated. On her, though, he liked it. A lot.

"Is this the part when things get awkward between us?" She gripped her phone by her side, her knuckles white.

"Only if we let them." He stood and crossed to her, noting the way her gaze dropped to his chest, then lower, to the already-returning bulge in his jeans. Hell, where she was concerned, he was like a teen who couldn't get enough.

"I thought you…" She licked her lips and nodded toward his erection.

He cleared his throat. "I did. You?"

Her cheeks pinkened. "What do you think?"

"I think you can no longer say you've never had an orgasm with a man."

She grinned and slammed her palm against his chest. "I don't think that counts."

Before she could pull away, he grabbed her hand and

tugged her toward him. "Did you come?"

Her flush grew deeper. "I don't recall any of your body parts doing the work."

"No?"

"No," she breathed, her eyes dropping to his mouth.

"My hands weren't there. I'll give you that. But my mouth and tongue—they definitely played a role in getting you off."

Her lips parted and her eyes grew darker. "You shouldn't be so cocky," she whispered. "If you'd been in there, I would have frozen up. That's what I do."

He growled and ran his fingers down the side of her neck. "You're not frozen now."

"This is different. There's no pressure. We're not going to have sex."

He trailed his fingers across her collarbone and dipped them into the top of the robe between her breasts.

Her breathing was ragged. "We aren't going to have sex, Ben."

"Are you trying to convince me or yourself?"

She stepped back and fisted the robe together at her neck. "Both."

He nodded. He was going to have to take this slow. They both wanted it. He just had to get Reese to accept the inevitable. "Then you better get dressed before I try to change your mind."

***

"There you are!" someone called through the crowd.

The lobby of the recital hall was packed with proud parents, aunts, and uncles, all waiting for the concert to begin, and Reese frowned as she tried to identify the source of the voice.

She spotted Tricia and pushed through the crowd to join her.

"Wait!"

Reese looked down to the fingers curled around her arm and then up to the face they belonged to. "Lance? What are you doing here?"

Lance's eyes went wide as she spun to face him. "God, look at you. You're stunning."

She felt a little satisfaction at that, but not enough to diminish her annoyance. "Why are you *here*?" According to her watch, she had five minutes to make her way into the auditorium before Sydney's concert would begin.

Lance tucked his hands into his pockets and gave a bashful smile. "We planned on coming together the day we found out she got to be in the band."

Reese gaped. "We planned on a lot of things. Marriage, babies, growing old together. Should I have made it clear that those were also off the table when you left me?"

He dropped his shoulders. "Don't be like this, Reese. I thought it would be nice to support Sydney together. She's important to me too."

Reese flinched. *Of course.* She rolled her shoulders. What was it Halie had said? *It's not always about you.* "Okay, let's get in there."

Adjusting her dress, Reese led the way into the auditorium. Sydney was already on stage with the rest of the band. Sitting at the glossy black baby grand, she stretched her thin fingers over the keys as she tested them.

Reese's heart tugged at the sight. God, she loved this kid.

Someone touched her shoulder. "Mind if I join you?"

Her heart stumbled at the sound of Ben's voice, but as she turned to take in his face, it full-out tripped, wiping out right there in the middle of the aisle and stealing the words from her lips. Sweet green eyes crinkled at the edges, and her fingers itched to run over his ever-present scruff.

Ben caught sight of Lance and his smile fell away. "Oh."

She swallowed and shook her head. She squeezed Ben's arm before he could escape. "I'd love your company," she said so Lance could hear. Then, softer, *"Please."*

Before their odd trio could take three more steps toward their destination, Mark was calling after her. "Wait up!"

Laughter bubbled up inside Reese as they settled into their

seats. The Hawk brothers bullied their way into the seats on either side of her and Lance slid into the seat directly behind her.

Lance leaned forward and brushed her hair away from her ear. "Hey."

At his touch, a shudder passed through her. As far as shudders went, this one was less touched-by-sexual-longing and more touched-by-sexual-predator.

"I can't get over how gorgeous you look."

"Thanks," she said woodenly.

Ben turned to her, blatantly ignoring Lance. "So, want to get a beer at Luke's place after? Maybe we can get Trish to tag along?"

"Sounds good." She needed the beer *now*.

Lance began massaging her shoulders and Reese snapped around, glaring. "Do not touch me."

Lance drew back. "I thought you missed me?"

Gaping. "You thought I *what*?"

"Lance, man," Mark said. "Take your creep factor down a notch."

Turning to the front again, Reese tried to make herself relax. She was biting back a maniacal giggle when Lance said, "Nothing changes, does it?"

She turned awkwardly in her seat. "Excuse me?"

"You're still following him around like a sick puppy," Lance said under his breath.

Lance had tried to share the words for her ears only, but Ben stiffened beside her.

"It's not your business anymore, Lance," she said.

Before she could say more, Ben caught her face in his hands and kissed her.

Warm lips against hers, the kiss was gentle and brief and relatively chaste, but it left her heart pounding and body wanting more. When he drew back, his eyes were hot on hers.

The crowd applauded as the band director took the stage. He signaled for silence and they began, the auditorium filling with the crooning beat of the jazz band.

Reese listened, aware of every move Ben made next to her, every breath he took. She wanted to be in his bedroom again, his body so close to hers, his eyes on her mouth as his fingers skimmed over her collarbone. She'd gotten dressed and gone home, but she wanted a do-over. Wanted to go back and take what the moment had offered them both.

She wanted. And she didn't want.

Ben leaned over and whispered, "She's amazing," his breath hot against her ear.

Sydney played with the passion and intensity of someone who had found her calling, her fingers flying over the keys. Sydney. An eighth-grader who knew exactly who she was and what she wanted. Reese envied that.

"I know," she said softly.

Ben reached for her hand, and when his fingers laced through hers, she didn't know if it was for his benefit or for Lance's. All she knew was how good it felt to have him by her side, how right it felt to have his calloused fingers twined through hers.

***

"You dirty, dirty slut!" Tricia screeched.

"You're just jealous you didn't get to see Lance's face," Reese protested between laughs.

"Damn straight," Trish said.

Ben grinned as the sisters sparred. Everyone had decided to come to the bar after Sydney's recital, and since Sydney had begged to have dinner with a friend, Tricia had gotten to come too.

"But Lancelot got the message?" Trish asked.

"I can only assume so," Reese said. "He slipped out before the end."

"Unfortunately, he was gone before I could do my part to help," Mark said.

Ben grunted. "Over my dead body."

"Well, on *that* note, I need another drink," Tricia said,

grabbing her purse. "Can I get the rest of you anything?"

Reese shook her head. "I'm done. I need to get going anyway."

"I'll go with you," Mark said to Tricia, pushing away from the table.

When Ben and Reese were alone, the silence stretched between them. Not awkward. Not tense. More like a long, bittersweet moment between lovers waiting for the right moment. That's all he needed with Reese. The right moment.

She'd let him hold her hand. He wasn't sure what it meant to her, but somehow it had felt more intimate to him than their time on her couch the night they met. More intimate than the words they'd exchanged on the phone last night.

With a forced smile, Reese withdrew an envelope from her purse and handed it to Ben. "Apparently, Sex Goddess equals dirty."

"Is this your next step?" He stifled a grin. "Please tell me she's making you burn your bras." He signaled to the door with his thumb. "I think I have some lighter fluid at the house."

"What? Of course she's not." She scowled. "I hope not."

Ben's eyes dropped south for a second. "You know, bras are a sign of repression. Liberate the breasts and liberate the woman."

She rolled her eyes. "Stop being a dork and read the letter."

Ben frowned. "You're taking this program more seriously than I thought you would."

Reese snorted. "No, I've just gotten really good at faking it."

"The new outfit doesn't look fake. Or the makeup."

Balls clacked at the pool table behind them and the Bears game played on the big screen.

"So, I like looking sexy. Women like to be wanted, Ben. It comes standard with the estrogen."

"And men didn't want you before you started taking Halie's Holy Steps?"

"Most of which I'm *faking*," she reminded him. She waved a

hand dismissively. "Just read it."

"The phone sex didn't seem fake," he said softly. Neither had her hand in his or the way she'd squeezed his hand when Sydney played her solo.

A red tinge crept up her cheeks. Satisfied, Ben turned to the letter.

Say goodbye to your panties. For the next week, you'll be going commando, forcing your mind to acknowledge the parts of your body too often left as an afterthought.

He grunted. "No wonder my guys want their wives to sign up."

"Spoken like a true male. Foregoing underwear isn't sexy, it's *unsanitary*."

He shook his head. "It's sexy."

"What if I'm doing yard work?"

"Sexy."

She crossed her arms and her cheeks flushed. "Or I'm working out?"

"Still sexy."

Reese leaned forward. "Or I want to wear a skirt?"

Ben narrowed his eyes. "Now you're just tormenting me."

She shook her head. "I don't need to go commando to acknowledge my female parts."

Leaning back in his chair, Ben folded his arms across his chest and studied her. Why was she taking this program so seriously? The kiss? The phone sex? He wasn't complaining, but couldn't she have just as easily fabricated a story for Halie?

They were the questions that were starting to niggle at him. Despite what Reese said, this was about more than a job.

He handed back the letter and only let himself ask one question. "So, when do the panties come off?"

CHAPTER FIFTEEN

Someone was lifting up her skirt.

Smacking away the unwelcome hands, Reese spun around, her coffee sloshing all over the floor. "What the—" She froze when she saw Halie, arms crossed, glaring at her.

Halie's manicured nails tapped her toned bicep. "Busted."

Reese closed her eyes, willing herself to disappear.

"These steps aren't optional. You either want to complete the program or you don't."

I don't. Even as Reese thought the words, she knew they weren't true. Because as much as she'd dreaded Halie's program and its steps, something was changing in her. And she liked it. Liked the way people looked at her, as if they were actually *seeing* her, as if before this program, people had only dismissed her. She liked the way *Ben* was looking at her.

She swallowed hard. "I've only been wearing underwear in public. When I'm at home alone—"

"Do you only want to be a Sex Goddess when you're at home alone?"

"That's a rhetorical question, right?"

Halie narrowed her eyes and Reese noticed for the first time that her boss looked like hell. Halie was dressed impeccably, as usual, but even her expensive concealer couldn't hide the dark circles under her eyes. Her carefully applied lip liner only accentuated her frown.

"I don't suppose this is a good time to tell you my progress on step six?"

"What?"

"Step six." Reese realized she was twisting her hands together and dropped them to her sides. "A date with a man I'd never marry. I have plans with Mark for this weekend."

Halie raised a brow. "Mark?"

Reese took a step back at the hardness in the woman's tone. "Mark Hawk."

Halie stepped to the counter and poured herself a cup of coffee. "His brother is your best friend, right?"

I think. "Yes."

"Do you want to be more?"

"With Mark?"

"With Ben."

"No. I mean, I didn't think so." She took a long sip of her coffee but it turned to dust in her mouth. She hadn't stopped thinking about Saturday night's phone conversation or the heat in Ben's eyes when she'd emerged from his bathroom. She hadn't stopped imagining what he must have looked like, hard shaft in his hand as he stroked himself and spoke the words that made her come.

And even though it was so innocent against the rest, she hadn't stopped thinking about the chaste kiss he'd given her in the middle of the auditorium or the way he'd held her hand.

"I don't know what I want." Reese bit her lip.

There hadn't been a reason for her to share the step about going without panties. It wasn't anything she needed his help with. It wasn't anything he needed to know. But she'd shared it anyway.

She'd wanted to hear what he'd say, sure. She knew he'd make her laugh. But, more, she'd done it because she'd wanted him to think about it. Next time he saw her, she wanted him to wonder what she wore under her skirt. She wanted him to run his eyes over her and grow hard. She wanted to be the first thing that came to his mind next time he wrapped his hand around himself, the last thing he thought about as he found his release.

She wanted Ben to want her. She wanted him to push the boundaries between them, and she wanted to let him.

Halie's lips curved up in a smile, and, for the first time, some light came into her eyes. "Well, there's your next step."

Reese looked around. What had she missed?

"Go have lunch with your friend today."

Reese frowned. "My next step is having lunch with my best friend?"

Halie's face softened. "Your face lights up when you talk about him. I know my program has a reputation for making women do crazy things, but it's really about giving women permission to be who they want to be. Your next step is having lunch with your friend because he brings you joy. It doesn't have to be complicated."

Reese's stomach flipped. Because it was complicated. Her mind and her heart and her libido were at odds with each other. She wanted Ben and she didn't. She wanted more from him and she didn't. She knew what was at stake if they went any further down this road, but she also knew how he made her feel. She knew he wanted her, but she also knew she'd spent years waiting for him. He'd never wanted her in return. Not until her makeover.

"Stop over-thinking it. It's just lunch."

"Just lunch."

"Yes." Halie grinned. "Lunch without panties."

***

"This house is gorgeous," Reese said as she followed Ben into his latest renovation. "I love the beams and the vaulted ceilings. Did you do that?"

"Sure did." His chest swelled with pride as he led her through the house.

When she'd texted and asked if he could meet her for

lunch, he suggested she come here. He'd wanted Reese to see this. She'd seen some of his work before, but never a project as extensive as this one. Her opinion had always mattered, but never quite this much. "It wasn't always like this. The house was built in the seventies so it was chopped up in a bunch of tiny rooms, walls everywhere, the kitchen isolated from the rest of the house."

"You'd never know," she said, turning a slow circle as they entered the kitchen. She moved her gaze to meet his and smiled. "Thanks for inviting me." She dropped her purse on the counter. "I needed to get out of that office."

"Trouble in Sex Goddess Paradise?"

She shook her head. "Halie's in a mood and I get the feeling she's the type that likes taking it out on someone." Her teeth sank into her plump bottom lip. He wanted to take that lip between his teeth and suck.

He let out a slow breath. "You hungry?"

"Not exactly." She gave an unsure smile. "I thought maybe we could talk."

His stomach burned. They had talked plenty since the night she'd used his tub, but they hadn't had *the talk*. "You know, guys don't like it when pretty girls say those words."

"You're not going to sweet talk your way out of this conversation, Ben."

Sure, but he couldn't just stand here, not when he wanted to press her against the fridge and put his mouth on her. Not when his hands itched to touch her, to feel the slick heat between her legs, to whisper dirty words like he had Saturday night, but this time while he could see her face.

Her phone buzzed from inside her purse, and she flinched. "That's probably for work."

"Turn it off for thirty minutes." He pulled the black handbag from the counter. "You deserve a break."

She smiled. "You do it. If I see anyone I recognize on the caller ID, I won't be able to resist."

He lifted the flap on her purse to retrieve her phone.

"Wait! Stop!"

Ben ignored the buzzing cell and pulled out a lace thong. He held it in two hands, examining. A grin tugged at his lips as her face fell.

"Shit," she muttered.

"You just cussed," he said, peering at her through the lace.

Her shoulders dropped. "Sorry."

"Why? Dirty looks good on you, Reese." He extended the panties toward her. "And I bet these do too. Do I want to know who was lucky enough to peel them off you?"

She hoisted herself up on the counter and crossed her ankles. "Halie McCormack."

He slammed his fist to his sternum and groaned. "Damn. I'd be jealous if I wasn't so turned on."

"Don't be a pig. What you're imagining is way sexier than the reality."

He crossed his arms. "Why do you have to do that? Was my little fantasy hurting anybody?"

Reese rolled her eyes. "She busted me for wearing underwear when I was supposed to be going commando."

All the blood left Ben's brain and traveled south. He dropped his gaze to her legs where her skirt had bunched around her thighs. He zeroed in on the spot where flesh met hem. "So if I slid my hand up your skirt right now…"

Reese's tongue darted out to wet her lips. "If you slid your hand up my skirt right now, you'd find something. But it wouldn't be panties." She spread her thighs an inch. Two.

An adjustment? An invitation?

Ben took a step toward her and placed his fingertips just above her knees. "You're wearing a skirt."

"Yes." Her throat moved as she swallowed. Her gaze shifted to his mouth.

"I thought you didn't like to wear skirts without underwear." He settled his thumbs on her inner thighs, just above her knees, and brushed lightly.

She shifted, sliding her hips forward on the counter, parting her legs infinitesimally. "I feel exposed," she whispered.

Ben's hands slid up an inch, thumbs still on inner thighs,

fingertips creeping toward the hem of her skirt. "You aren't," he said, focusing on the V in her legs concealed by her skirt. "Not yet. They'd show this on primetime TV."

She shifted again, leaning back a bit as she slid her hips forward. The hem of the skirt raised another inch, bringing it damn near the top of her thighs. When she opened her legs further, he stopped breathing.

"What about now?" she asked.

"Close," he managed, his voice sounding thick to his own ears. "You're almost to cable." He let his hands slide another inch higher and her breathing hitched. "I think you should try for late-night Cinemax."

Reese settled her hands between her legs at the edge of the counter. Slowly, she shimmied left and right until the skirt up bunched high around her hips. Only then did she part her thighs. "Would this do the trick?"

He couldn't help the way his fingers curled into her flesh, the way his thumbs traveled further up the path of soft flesh. She was exposed just enough. And she wasn't just beautiful, she was aroused. Looking at Reese, this intimate piece of her body, this wasn't something he'd forget. "This should get you through your opening scene."

She pressed into his touch, an invitation. "And what happens next?"

Ben's cock ached and pressed against his zipper. "Now or on Cinemax?" He tore his gaze away from the swollen flesh between her legs and met her gaze.

"Cinemax," she said, cheeks flushed. "What happens next there?"

"You'd be fucked silly." His eyes landed on her swollen bottom lip as she pulled it through her teeth. "Hard, fast, thorough."

"And what about now?" She put her hand on top of his and pressed it into her inner thigh. "Same thing?"

Ben would have smiled, but he couldn't. "Not a chance."

She pulled back and he held her fast.

"I wouldn't dare rush this, Reese." His eyes locked on hers

as he found her wet, exposed sex with the pad of his thumb. "I've been thinking about it too long to rush it." He brushed over her clit, watched her eyes flash to his and grow darker. She shifted again, moving closer to his hand.

He slid a finger inside her and watched as pleasure transformed her features. Her lids drifted closed. Her head tilted back slightly. Her chest rose and fell as her breathing grew shallow. He pumped his fingers inside her, and his cock pulsed as he imagined how this tight, wet heat would feel wrapped around his dick.

He withdrew his finger and she gasped, curving her hips for more. He slid two inside her and stepped between her legs. With his other hand, he grabbed her ass and pulled her close as he moved his fingers.

"Look at me."

She opened her eyes and the heat there nearly undid him. How could this woman believe she was cold?

"You're so beautiful when you're turned on."

Rocking her hips into his hand, she ran a thumb over his bottom lip. He took it into his mouth, biting lightly.

He wanted to kiss her, to taste her, but he didn't dare miss a moment of the pleasure tracking across her features. "I love watching you," he said into her ear. "I'm going to love every minute of making you come."

She tensed in his arms. "I can't."

"You can."

She shook her head against him. "It's too much pressure."

"Relax," he whispered. He dragged his lips over her neck, tasting her, sucking at that tender skin. "We're not worrying about that today."

She straightened. "I'm sorry. It's so pathetic. I just—"

He cut her off with his mouth. He kissed her until her shoulders dropped, kissed her until her lips opened under him, kissed her until she moaned into his mouth. Only then, when her body turned supple, did he move his hand again.

He circled her clit. "You like that."

She peered up at him through her thick lashes. "Yes, but I

can't—"

"Don't you dare come."

She curled her fingers into his shoulder blades and her wet heat squeezed his fingers. "What?"

"I want you slick and wet. I want you right at the edge. I want you to spend the rest of your day thinking about me." His lips brushed her ear as he spoke.

Outside, he heard the rumble of a diesel engine pulling into the drive.

They were about to have company.

***

Halie tapped her pencil on her desk and looked at her notes, but they blurred in front of her eyes. She couldn't see a thing but that woman—that tiny little thing in knock-off Jimmy's and a bad dye job.

But Alex hadn't given a shit about the girl's bad taste in clothes and stylists. All he'd cared about was the woman's mouth on his cock.

He'd wanted Halie to walk in on them. He'd wanted her to see.

She'd opened the door and met his eyes and they'd flared hot, then his hand had tightened in the girl's hair. Not because he thought Halie would join them. He knew better. He was setting the precedent, letting her know this was how it was going to be if they married.

She rubbed the bridge of her nose and snatched her phone off its receiver. "Quinn, could you get me Reese Regan's file?"

"Her HR file or her client file?"

"Client."

Something about Reese's relationship with Ben was sitting wrong with her.

"Here you go," Quinn said, handing her a manila folder.

"Do you remember what her romantic background is?"

"She just got out of a long-term relationship with a man named Lance. Six months ago? They lived together and it ended badly."

Halie leaned back and crossed her arms. "Did she end it or did he?"

"He did." Quinn looked down at her notes. "One night she came home from work and he was packing his things. He told her he couldn't live with a sexual ice queen another day." She grunted. "What an ass."

"Is she going to find herself in the same situation with this best friend of hers? Is he going to hurt her?"

Quinn shifted and looked at her shoes. "Ben's different, I think."

She held up her hand. "Let's find out a little more, shall we?" Halie hit the speaker button on her phone and dialed Tricia.

"Halie!" Tricia crooned by way of greeting. "Sydney is staying with a friend this weekend. Please tell me you're calling because you want to go out."

Halie smiled. A little girl time would do her good. "Sure, but that's not why I'm calling."

"What's up?"

"Your sister—why haven't she and Ben ever hooked up?"

Tricia was silent a long moment, then, "They have. A long time ago."

"A puzzle piece revealed," Halie said, looking at Quinn. "And why not since?"

"It was six years ago, when they first met. She's moved past it. And, anyway, now she has the hots for Mark."

Halie frowned, remembering Reese's crush and the sexist jock radio personality. Hadn't he agreed to take Reese out? Right, Reese had said he was her step six. If that was true, she couldn't be all that interested in him. "You said she moved past it. What about Ben?"

"He just wanted to be friends. Though it seems to me he feels differently these days." Trish sighed audibly. "I know it sounds crazy."

"No, it sounds like something you're not telling me."

"Listen, they don't talk about it. I don't want to—"

"My lips are sealed."

Trish was quiet for several long moments. "Ben and Reese hooked up when they first met. Just one hot night. He showed up at her apartment and they went at each other."

"They had sex?"

"No, but they messed around. Reese liked him. A lot."

"And then?"

"Ben found out his ex died while he was there fooling around with Reese. He wasn't even a week out of a three-year relationship, and he hooks up with this new girl—Reese—and his phone is ringing like crazy. Calls and texts all coming from the ex's number. He figured she was trying to get ahold of him and make more excuses for cheating. He ignored the calls and found out later it was Lisa's mom trying to get a hold of him. Lisa was in the hospital, dying from injuries she'd sustained in a car accident."

"Damn," Halie muttered.

"He was grieving, you know? So Reese gave him space and time. She waited. They became great friends and she let him grieve. She waited for him to heal and take their relationship back to the place where it had started. We all thought it was only a matter of time."

"But he never did. Did she tell him how she felt?"

"It was over a year after Lisa died, and I told her she needed to make the first move. She took my advice."

Halie looked at Quinn, whose eyes had gone wide.

"What happened?" Quinn asked.

Tricia was quiet again, as if reliving the memory herself. "I think he was just scared, you know? He and Reese were so close by then."

"What happened?" Halie asked this time.

"He broke her heart."

CHAPTER SIXTEEN

Reese clung to Ben as he added light friction to her clit. "I want you to spend the rest of your day wondering if I could have gotten you off. I want your mind on my fingers and my mouth."

Jesus. She was so close. On the counter. With *Ben*.

"You're gorgeous when you're turned on," Ben whispered, his hot breath against her ear.

Ben stood between her legs, his hand doing deliciously naughty things to her, pumping his fingers in and out of her.

Someone pounded on the front door.

Reese registered the sound and straightened.

"Boss? The door's locked."

"Be there in a sec!" Ben called. He cupped her sex softly and groaned against the side of her neck.

"We never got to talk." She sounded breathless to her own ears. Ben was right, she wouldn't think about anything else all day.

"You wanted to talk about us?"

She nodded. "I don't know what we're doing. We agreed a long time ago—"

"Boss!"

"On my way," Ben called. He turned back to Reese, eyes

hot as they ran over her. "Come over tonight."

"To talk?"

"To get naked, Reese. That's my plan. I'm getting you naked tonight, but there can be talking too"—his lips drew up in a grin—"since you seem to like that."

Her breath caught and she forced herself to relax. "I don't know what we're doing, but Ben"—she curled her fingers into his shirt and nuzzled her face into his neck, breathing in his scent—"I don't want to stop."

Withdrawing his hand from between her legs, he groaned. "Me neither."

He helped her off the counter, and her body slid against his as he settled her to the ground. He was hard. And impressive.

He squeezed her hand. "Unless you're not opposed to an audience, I'm going to have to."

Her cheeks burned. "That's not what I mean."

Steps sounded in the hall and Reese froze.

"There a reason you locked the door in the middle of the day?" a man called out in a grumble. One of Ben's carpenters came around the corner. He spotted Reese and stopped in his tracks. "Oh." Looking between Reese and Ben, a knowing grin split his face. "Sorry, boss."

Ben strategically positioned himself behind the counter, and Reese had to swallow her laughter as she realized he was hiding his erection.

"Frank, this is Reese Regan, my…"

Reese waited to hear his label for her. His what? His friend? That title hardly seemed sufficient, considering all the awkwardness in the air.

He never finished his sentence. Reese figured Frank had the general idea anyway. "Reese, this is Frank, one of my crew leaders."

Reese's cheeks warmed as Frank nodded. "Really nice to meet you, Reese." He gestured toward the door. "I think I'll just wait outside." He winked at Reese before the echo of his steel-toed boots carried him out the front of the house.

When he was gone, she pressed her hands to her cheeks.

"Oh, my God, I'm so sorry. He's going to think—"

Ben took her hands in his and drew them to her sides. "What? That we were in here making out like a couple of horny teenagers?"

She bit her lip. "That's kind of how I feel."

"Good," he growled. "I'd hate to be the only one."

"This is crazy."

"Is it?" He ran his thumb over her bottom lip.

She wanted him to suck it into his mouth, wanted his fingers in her body again.

"When you said you didn't want to stop, what did you mean?"

Her heart pounded, and it was there, that horrible fear that he might reject her again, that horrible memory of him telling her he didn't want more.

Unapologetically pursue the life you want.

"Ben, I like this. I like the flirting and…" He stared at her, and she swallowed back her self-consciousness. "I like when you touch me."

He traced the line of her jaw and down the side of her neck. "I like touching you," he said, his voice thick.

"I don't want to stop." She licked her lips. Somehow, it was easy to ask for sex, but anything more terrified her. She dropped her gaze to the floor. "I don't want to pretend we're nothing more than friends."

"Good." Then his mouth was on hers and his hands were in her hair as he kissed her hard. It wasn't a gentle kiss of seduction, it was a demanding kiss of branding, claiming, possessing.

When he pulled away, her breath came short and shallow and her legs were putty.

Sighing, she leaned back and let the wall support her.

He stayed close and put a hand on either side of her head, his mouth was so close it almost brushed hers as he spoke. "Let me see you tonight?"

She closed her eyes at the pleasure that rushed through her at his words. "I promised Masey we'd go shopping, but I can come over after."

His eyes were on her mouth. Was he thinking about where he wanted it? What she would do with it she got him alone and naked? Because she was and the sooner—

"Not tonight, then."

What? "You're going to make me wait?"

The side of his mouth tilted up in a grin. "Oh, yeah. I'm going to make you wait, and I'm going to make you think about it. Familiar with delayed gratification?" He leaned close so he spoke against her ear. "I want you to need me so badly you beg."

She bit her bottom lip to keep herself from doing just that. "Tomorrow?"

He groaned against her neck. "I promised my mom I'd come over for dinner." He trailed kisses along the side of her neck, and his hand slipped under her skirt, cupping her bare, swollen sex. When he slid his fingers inside her, the movement was sudden and thick and deep.

She gasped. "After?" The word came out more a whimper than a question.

At the front of the house, two men were talking in low tones, and one of them laughed. She heard the slamming of doors, the muffled sound of someone giving orders.

"Not enough time," Ben said. "When I get you naked, I'm going to need *hours.*"

Inside her, he crooked his fingers and found a spot that—

"Oh my God." She clung to him, rocked her hips. He pressed closer until she was pinned between him and the wall, his hand between them, his fingers working inside her.

She drew a leg up around him, bunching her skirt at her hips and sending his fingers deeper.

Outside, more doors slammed as the crew returned, more low chuckling.

"Do you have any idea what you look like right now?" The words came out a low rumble against her ear. "Your eyes dark and wild, your leg wrapped around me? You have any idea how sexy you are when you're turned on?"

"Where are you heading with those?" a voice called from out front.

"We have to stop," Reese said weakly, but she couldn't bring herself to push him away. "We should—"

"Nah, just the porch for now." Another deep voice. Closer now.

"You like it," Ben growled against her ear. "You like knowing someone could walk in here any minute." He shifted his hand and found her clit with his thumb.

"Ben." She wanted and she didn't want. But his fingers, and his voice, and she couldn't—

"You like the idea of someone seeing you like this—hot and needy, and ready to be fucked."

"God," she breathed.

"Another time, baby, after I've had you to myself, long and slow, I'll bring you back here." His hand moved faster, his fingers moved harder, touching something deeper and tender and—

"I'll put you on the counter while we have the place to ourselves. I'll spread your legs and lick you."

Another slam of a car door. "Boss is in there?"

"Then when they start coming back from lunch, I'll take you against this wall."

She didn't want that, did she? But his fingers, and the fantasy, and his voice, and this was *so good*.

Outside, more boots on gravel.

"You'll wonder if we'll be caught, if someone will find out this secret side of you. This is you, Reese. Hot and sexy and a little bit wild. It's always been you."

"Ben…" She felt it coming, clung to him as the pleasure climbed and her muscles contracted around his fingers.

"Don't fight it." He breathed the words, his voice sounding as tense as she felt. "Let yourself go. Let yourself be that sexy, amazing woman you are, the woman who doesn't care if someone sees, the woman who's going to let me fuck her against this wall."

The front door squeaked. "Boss? You ready for us?"

She bit his shoulder and let go. Her whole body quaked and shuddered as the orgasm tore through her.

"Boss?"

"Man, back the fuck off," someone called from the front.

Ben groaned against her neck. "I don't know whether to kill them or thank them," he grumbled. His hand was still between her legs and, as he withdrew it, she whimpered a little. He might have too.

"I can't believe I just did that," she whispered.

His lip twitched up in a lopsided grin. "Which part?"

Her cheeks burned. "All of it."

"You're a natural." He tucked her hair behind her ear and settled her to the ground. "Come with me tomorrow. Mom would like to see you."

"You want me to be in the same room with your mom next time I see you?"

"Delayed gratification. You'll thank me."

She licked her lips. "Can I trust you to be on good behavior?"

He dropped his eyes to her body, to the hem of her skirt, which had fallen to her knees. "I guess that depends on what you wear under your skirt."

***

Masey looked like someone had run over her dog, and she was flicking through the racks of Nordstrom like the clothes were personally responsible for her loss.

At first, Reese had been worried. Since Reese had met her their freshman year of college, she'd known Masey to be positive and upbeat. If she was upset, there was a good reason.

But after an hour of shopping with Miss Grumpy Pants, Reese had no more information about the source of the woman's misery and was beginning to grow irritated.

Masey huffed. "There's nothing I want here. Let's go somewhere else." Without waiting for a response, she turned on her heel and headed out of the store.

Crossing her arms, Reese followed her friend.

This was what she was doing instead of going to Ben's and letting him strip her bare? *This* was how she was spending her evening when Ben could be using his hands and his mouth and—

"Spill it."

Masey snapped her head up, her eyes less "woman scorned" and more "lost puppy."

"What?"

Reese softened. "What's wrong?"

She shook her head. "It's nothing." She pointed to a little boutique. "Want to go in there?"

Normally, Reese steered clear of places that catered to the Halie McCormacks of the world. If the price tags didn't make her feel inferior enough, her fashion cluelessness finished the job. But, thanks to Halie, her bank account was a little healthier and her fashion sense a little stronger. "Sure. Let's see what we can find."

At the front of the store, a mannequin wore a red satin gown that made Reese pause. Her fingers itched to touch it. What would Ben think of this dress? Could she even pull it off? The fabric looked like it would cling to her curves and give away every imperfection. Even with her newly adventurous sense of style, she wasn't ready for that.

"I'm sorry I've been such a bitch," Masey muttered.

Reese nodded, thought of Halie saying, *"Don't say it's okay when it's not. You're telling people, with every word out of your mouth, how they can treat you."*

"Thank you for the apology," she said simply.

"It's just man trouble. I found out my crush has a crush and it's not me." Masey held up a hand. "And before you ask, no I don't want to talk about it. He's not worth the time."

"O-*kay*."

Masey blew out a breath. "You probably wish you never said you'd come shopping with me."

"Well, maybe, but only because I'd rather be naked with Ben."

As her eyes widened, some of the misery left Masey's face. "What?" She grabbed Reese's arm and dragged her to a dressing room, closing the door behind them. "Give me details!"

"Can I help you with anything?" a small, squeaky voice called on the other side of the door.

Reese reached to unlock the door only to have her hand smacked away.

Masey crossed her arms. "I'll wait here all day if I have to."

"You don't have to wait all day. I'd be happy to get you another size, another item?" the bewildered voice on the other side of the door called.

"My friend's a size fourteen," Masey called. "Find her something she can have peeled off her...by her new *lover*." She emphasized the word and jabbed her finger in Reese's direction.

"Well," said the voice outside their dressing room. "Just one second."

Masey tapped her foot, waiting.

Reese bit back a smile. "Some things have happened," she hedged.

"Such as?"

"Phone sex."

Masey's eyes went wide. "Seriously? How was it?"

There were no words, at least not ones she was willing to share. Except maybe, "Dirty."

"How dirty?"

"X-rated."

"Was this one of your steps?"

She slanted her gaze at Masey. "I might have implied it was."

"You *lied* to get Ben to have phone sex with you?" she shrieked.

Reese nudged her. "Keep your voice down!" Then, softer, "I'd had some wine, and I was using his tub. He called my cell, I answered. It happened."

A stream of deep red satin floated over the dressing room

door. "Try this and let's see what you think."

Masey whistled. "That's hot."

Reese stood up and fingered the red satin that was draped over the door. "Then, today, I went to his job site for lunch, and…" She drew in a shaky breath. *And he made me come my brains out.* "I think we're going to try to make this work."

A squeak sounded on the other side of the door. "It will be perfect on you."

The material kissed her fingertips and Reese imagined the dress would feel as silky on as the lingerie she'd picked out with Ben.

"Did you tell him you lied?"

Reese met Masey's eyes. "I didn't lie. Not really."

Masey put her hands on her hips. "You need to start this right, Reese. Tell him the truth."

"I need a minute." Reese pushed Masey out of the dressing room and shut the door. Once she was alone, she removed her clothes and stood naked, staring at the dress. Was Ben at home now? Was he thinking of her?

She pulled the dress over her head, letting it slide like cool water over her skin. She didn't bother looking in the mirror, but the air danced against her back, so she peeled off her bra before stepping out of the dressing room.

Reese recognized the first "Oh!" as the squeak of the dressing room attendant, and the sigh of "Oh, Reese" as Masey's voice, but she didn't look at either of them. Instead, she walked directly to the three mirrors ahead of her and looked at herself.

The dress itself was beautiful, a deep apple-red satin that floated down her body and touched the floor. But what took her breath away was the way she looked in it. The cowl neck drooped to show off her delicate collarbone. She ran her fingertips over the skin there, realizing for the first time how sexy that spot on her body was. The satin draped over her until it reached her hips, where the material seemed to be cut to match the lines of her body until it flared at the bottom. She ran her hands over her hips and her heart beat a little faster.

Her hips were her most abhorred body part, and this dress showcased them like her greatest asset, accentuating the curve from her waist to hip, the full rounding of her rear. She turned slightly in the mirror to survey the back of the dress, which was cut all the way down to the base of her spine.

Ben would love this. Even now, she could imagine his eyes running over her, his fingers skipping along her spine as they traced the way to the small of her back.

"Sexy," Masey said.

Reese turned to the dressing room attendant, a short woman with a blond bob. "It is beautiful. I just don't know where I'd wear it." Even as the words left her mouth, she knew. She needed an outfit for the masquerade ball, and this dress was just the thing.

"Well, if I looked like that in that dress," the attendant said, "I have a feeling I'd wear it around the house, to the movies, even grocery shopping."

Reese searched for the price tag under her arm. Her jaw dropped at the numbers. Even with her new salary. "I can't swing that. I'm so sorry."

The woman's grin widened. "It's last season's style, so it's on clearance."

How much could she afford to blow on a dress she may only wear once?

"Seventy percent off," the attendant said.

Reese grinned. "Sold!" In the mirror, she caught sight of Masey's tenuous smile. "You okay, Mase?"

"I'm happy for you. You deserve a good relationship."

Reese turned to the attendant. "I'll be up front to pay for this in a few."

Getting the point, the woman nodded and left them alone.

"I don't think I'd call it a relationship. Not yet at least," Reese said softly. "I don't know what it is."

"You think you're just, what? Fuck buddies?"

The term made Reese wince. Because it was accurate or because that was what she was afraid of? "I think I need to be careful," she finally said.

Masey stepped forward and smoothed invisible wrinkles from the sides of Reese's dress. "Careful about what?"

"I don't want to hurt him." That was it. The fact she'd been avoiding. She wanted Ben, had never stopped wanting him, but what he didn't know about her mistakes would kill him. Not that she could explain that to Masey. She hadn't told anyone about that night with Mark.

"If you don't want to hurt him, you need to be honest with him."

Reese studied herself in the mirror, half in love with the dress. "I'll tell him the phone sex wasn't a step, but I really don't think he's going to care."

"That's not what I'm talking about."

Reese turned to see Masey frowning.

"You need to tell him you had sex with Mark."

CHAPTER SEVENTEEN

When Reese climbed into Ben's truck on Thursday night, his eyes immediately dropped to her denim-clad legs.

"Jeans?" He said it like it was a dirty word.

She clicked her seatbelt into place before looking at him. The heat in his eyes made her want to climb across the seat and straddle him, so it was probably better that she was restrained. "We're going to your parents' house. If I wore a skirt, you wouldn't behave."

He ran his eyes over her again, muttering, "I don't want to behave."

She reached over to put her hand on his thigh. "Then have me over tonight."

He grinned. "Been thinking about it?"

God, had she. "Maybe."

He put the truck into gear. "Keep thinking, and by tomorrow night…"

The only thing that kept her from whimpering and begging him to reconsider was her pride, and she wasn't sure how long that would hold up.

When Ben merged into traffic, Reese pulled her hand away, but he grabbed it and laced his fingers through hers. They rode like that, in silence, the hunger, lust, and tension crackling between them. And there was something else too, something that had nothing to do with sex, something comforting and *right* about the feel of his warm hand against hers.

By the time he parked the truck in his parents' paved driveway, she was wishing she *had* worn the skirt. She would have had him pull over at a rest area, would have crawled into his lap, skirt bunched around her hips, slid her hand between their bodies, and stroked him until he surrendered and slid into her.

But she didn't have a skirt on, and whatever game Ben was playing seemed to require he torture her at all costs. As it was, she was nearly panting with arousal from what her mind had conjured.

He faced forward until he'd turned off the ignition and unbuckled. Only then did he turn to her.

"Are you thinking what I'm thinking?" she asked.

"I assume you're not talking about Ma's lasagna?" He was grinning, but his eyes held something much more intense— much hotter—than a smile.

"Let me come over tonight," she said.

He leaned to her and in the next moment his mouth was on hers, his hands in her hair as his tongue parted her lips.

She opened under him, kissed him, tasted him, clung to his shirt and needed him. His hand found her breast, and she moaned against his mouth, pulled herself closer. When he latched onto her neck, it was all she could do not to crawl into his lap. She wanted him. Wanted this. Now.

His hand was between her legs, resting against the denim. "Are you wearing panties?" His voice like gravel against her ear.

"No."

He groaned, pressed harder, and the seam of her jeans rubbed her swollen clit.

"Not here, Ben." Even as she said it, she rocked her hips, wanting this, wanting more. He sucked at her lips, assaulted her mouth with his teeth, soothed with his tongue.

At some point, he'd gotten a hand up her shirt. His fingers

were teasing her nipple when someone pounded on the window.

Reese jumped back in her seat. Mark stood outside the window, a crooked smile on his face.

Ben took his time pulling away. Slowly, he hit the button to lower the window.

Reese did her best to straighten her clothes and smooth her hair, but there was no helping the flush on her cheeks.

"Enjoy the show?" Ben called when the window was half down.

Mark smirked. "Thought you'd like to know Ma was looking out from the kitchen, checking on you." With that, he stepped away from the car, waiting several yards away and toying with his phone.

"Shit."

The window hummed as Ben returned it to its closed position.

Reese studied him, the horror coloring his features. "You didn't want her to know about us," she said softly. She wasn't sure why it hurt so much. It wasn't like they were an item. They were just exploring. That wasn't something you told your mother.

He dragged a hand through his hair, blew out a slow breath. "I don't care if my mom knows, but I didn't want to hear a lecture on how she didn't raise her son to disrespect women."

"You were disrespecting me?" Heck, she needed a little more disrespect in her life.

"I'm pretty sure my truck isn't on my mom's list of approved locations to show a woman, er, *respect*."

Reese bit her lip. "I see."

"Let me go in first, okay? This is a lecture I'd prefer to get in private." He reached for the door.

"Could you…" She swallowed. "Could you somehow indicate that I'm not normally like this?"

He raised a brow. "You want me to lie to my mother?"

She smacked him in the chest. His warm, *solid* chest. She really needed to get him naked. ASAP. "It's not my fault you're

154

making me crazy by making me wait."

"You're right." He opened the door. "I'll explain that it's my fault. I won't have sex with you, and as a result you can't keep your hands off me."

"Ben!" she screeched.

But he winked at her and swung his door shut. "Got it."

She watched him go, feeling irritated and amused and embarrassed and still oh-my-God turned on.

Mark opened her door. "I guess this means our date's off," he said, tucking his hands into his pockets and looking sheepish.

"What?" Then she remembered. Saturday. Dinner, movie, Mark, step six. "Oh, crap on a cracker."

"I didn't really believe him when he said he wasn't interested in more with you. Wishful thinking, I guess."

Her heart sank a little. "Ben said that? When?"

He lifted a shoulder. "I don't know. Dad's retirement party? He insisted you were just friends, and I thought maybe it was time to make my move."

Mr. Hawk's retirement party had been before her makeover. Of course. She shouldn't be surprised, should she? She knew things had changed since then, and she'd known he hadn't wanted her before.

Then why did it hurt so damn much?

She grabbed her purse and climbed out of the truck. They ambled toward the house, trying to give Ben time.

"I figured," Mark said, "if you agreed to go out with me, Ben would either realize what an idiot he was being, or I'd get a real chance. Frankly, I was hoping for the second."

She worried her lip between her teeth. "Any chance you'd still be willing to go on that date?"

He stopped. "What?"

"I was hoping our date could still happen. If you don't mind."

His dark eyes narrowed in on her. "What are you playing at, Reese?"

She cringed. "It's kind of one of my steps."

He raised a brow. "Going out with me is one of your steps?"

"Going out with a man I'd never marry is one of my steps."

He winced.

"I'm sorry, Mark, but..." She was a world-class bitch. She blew out a breath. "You're a really good guy, you know I think so. But the way I feel about you...it's never been like that."

He nodded, tucked his head. "Yeah, I guess I knew that already." He studied her for a moment. "But my brother, he wouldn't qualify for this date you need to go on?"

From the Hawks' front walk, she looked into the house and spotted Ben. He smiled and waved her in. "I don't know," she said, something tugging in her chest.

"I'll do it," Mark said with a resigned sigh, "but only because I'm a fucking saint."

She grinned. "You are. Thank you."

He looked thoughtful for a minute, then added, "But you need to tell Ben. The man deserves fair warning before my good looks and charm bringing you to your senses."

She huffed. "I'm having enough trouble getting him naked. If you don't mind, I think I'll leave out the pillow talk about my fake date with his brother."

Mark made a face. "Okay, two things. First, I'd like to be spared any future details about your sex life with Ben."

"What sex life? He's torturing me. What is this 'delayed gratification' crap?"

Mark held up a hand, looking pained. "Second," he said firmly, "our date isn't the only thing you need to be honest with him about."

Reese sighed. "Yeah, and I guess I should get to that conversation soon since you can't seem to keep our secret to yourself."

His eyes widened, then he squeezed them shut. "Masey?"

"Yeah, Masey. Anyone else you told that I should know about?"

He shook his head. "No. I was feeling lovesick and she listened."

She crossed her arms. "What does you feeling lovesick have to do with this?" He just looked at her, and it hit her all at once. *Lovesick.* "You really *liked me*?"

He rocked back on his heels, set his jaw. "Not like I tried to hide it, Reese." He shook his head. "I might have a reputation as a chauvinist who's just after a piece of ass, but I've been sick of that game for a long time. I've wanted you for a long time, and I wouldn't have asked you out if I wasn't interested."

He stared at her and something clawed at her chest. She mocked the intelligence of women who failed to take Mark Hawk seriously, who failed to see there was more to him than his radio personality, and yet she herself was guilty. She hadn't believed she was worth wanting, so she hadn't seen that Mark wanted her.

Then he added, softly, "I wouldn't have slept with you that night if I hadn't hoped for more. Reese, you're the most amazing woman I know. You're sweet and caring and gorgeous and—"

"Mark." She had to make him stop. Each word was damning, making her feel worse, making her face her own mistakes. But what could she say? That she'd thought too little of him to believe she'd meant more than any other woman willing to go home with him that night? That she thought too little of him to believe a date would ever *lead* anywhere? "I'm sorry."

He shook his head. "Nah, it's not like I didn't know you wanted Ben. It's just…" He let out a long breath. "Halie McCormack came to me when you started her program."

Reese stepped back. "She did?"

"She asked me to go out with you, to pursue you." He laughed, but it was a dark sound without humor. "It was kind of like asking an addict to take another hit. Something I already wanted but had denied myself since the morning you woke up panicked in my bed."

"Oh, Mark, I swear I had no idea."

"Yeah, I know. I just hoped she knew something I didn't. I thought maybe you were coming around. I thought maybe I had a chance."

How was this even happening? How had she been so stupid? So blind? And it hurt to admit, but she'd been shallow. She'd been so busy thinking of Mark as the hot stud, she hadn't bothered to consider his feelings.

Mark kicked a loose piece of mulch back into the flowerbed. "Just promise me I get the honor of kicking his ass if he hurts you."

The front door opened, and they both jerked their attention to the sound.

Ben peeked out. "You two coming in?"

"I'm sorry," she said, looking at Mark, the restrained emotions pulling at his features. "I didn't know."

The screen bounced shut behind Ben as he stepped onto the porch. He narrowed his eyes at his brother. "Everything okay out here?"

"Yeah," Mark said, giving her a curt nod before heading toward the door. "Reese was just filling me in on the details of that bachelor auction she asked me to be in."

Ben's expression relaxed. "Oh, do you still need me to do that?"

She swallowed. "If you can, that would be a big help. Halie's having SG 101 graduates be the bachelorettes, but finding guys hasn't been nearly as simple."

"Whatever you need," Ben said softly as she climbed on the porch. He tucked her hair behind her ears and pressed a kiss to her lips. "I mean it."

"Thank you," she said, but guilt and doubt knotted together in her stomach as she followed him inside.

Even after Lance had left and she'd told herself she wanted Mark, her heart had belonged to Ben. Mark had been her security blanket, her lie, her excuse as she told herself she could be friends with Ben without going back to her puppy dog days of waiting for Ben to notice her.

Mark was the distraction, the one she never had to worry would hurt her, yet she'd hurt him. And Ben? Ben hadn't wanted her until she'd been fantastically made over. She couldn't blame him for that. She understood it, intellectually at least.

But if she let herself think about it too much, she'd have to acknowledge the scar that was there, a thick, knotty painful rift right in the foundation of any romantic relationship they'd ever have.

***

Ben hadn't had sex in over six months. He hadn't been interested since Reese had shown up at the PitStop, asked for three shots of tequila, and announced that Lance had left her. He planned to end that streak tonight. He planned to be with Reese tonight.

Ben snuck a glance at his watch as Halie toured his latest remodel. He'd been on his way out the door when she'd shown up asking to take a look.

He'd wanted to tell her *no*. He'd wanted to push her into her car so he could go home and seduce the hell out of his best friend. Since the future of Hawk Construction depended on her business, he'd resisted that temptation. Barely.

"I looked at your quote," Halie said, running her finger along the new granite countertops.

"And…?"

"And I called some references. Everyone seems to love Hawk Construction."

Ben did his best to keep his body language neutral and not pant like a hopeful puppy. "I'm glad to hear it."

"Of course, the company has never taken on a job like mine."

He tensed. Hell, this wasn't news to him. He knew the hardest part would be *breaking in* to the high-end market. No one wanted to be the first, no one wanted to be the guinea pig. "Since I've taken over the company from my father, I've been working on shifting the focus to larger projects. We're in transition, it's true."

"How do you think Reese is handling my program?"

159

LEXI RYAN

Ben rubbed his neck—this woman could give a guy whiplash with the way she changed subjects. "She's doing great."

"What do you think of her makeover?"

The hair stood up on his arms. Something told him to back away from the conversation. "She looks amazing."

"It's more than just how she looks. It's about how she feels." She shook her head. "She's a tougher case than I anticipated."

"Maybe because she didn't come to you an empty shell." Ben set his jaw. He needed to be kind to this woman, but her assumptions that Reese even *needed* that ridiculous program got under his skin. "Reese is plenty sexy."

Halie crossed her arms. "Of course she is. I wouldn't bother if I didn't believe that. But she doesn't believe it. Not yet."

Ben didn't reply. It wasn't like he was going to tell her about having Reese up against the wall, panting in his ear. He wasn't going to share that Reese had seemed pretty damn secure in her own appeal while he'd be been whispering dirty words and fucking her with his fingers.

Halie pulled a set of keys out of her purse and jangled them in her closed fist. "I'm taking a risk if I put you on this renovation."

"You won't regret it."

"If I do this, it would be to help your business move into new territory." She held the keys out to him.

Ben took them, cautiously.

"In return, I'd like you to help *my* business."

There it was again—that feeling that he didn't want to be part of this conversation, that this woman was dangerous and conniving.

"Would you be willing to do that?"

Ben gripped the keys until they bit into his palm. He crossed his arms. "What do you have in mind?"

Her smile was slick and cold. "Nothing you haven't already been thinking about."

He set his jaw. *She wouldn't.*

"Reese just needs a little push. A night with the man she's been pining after for years? That could be the perfect solution."

He tossed the keys back to her, and she snatched them from the air. "I appreciate the opportunity to take the job, but I keep my personal life and business life separate."

"Just think of it as me giving you permission to do something you want to do anyway."

"I don't need your permission for anything."

She raised a brow at that, then placed the keys on the counter and walked away.

The slam of the front door echoed through the house. The damn keys stared at him.

His jaw ached from clenching it. His body ached from wanting Reese.

And Halie McCormack had just fucked up everything.

His cell rang.

"Hawk," he answered shortly.

"Hey, you."

Ben closed his eyes at the sound of her voice, soft and sexy and—hell, if those two words could be *suggestive*, hers were. "Reese."

"I was getting ready to leave the office for the night. Want to know what I'm wearing under my skirt?"

Stifling a groan, he scooped Halie's keys off the counter. "You know I do."

"I'm planning to come over and let you find out."

He felt like he was being backed into a corner, and he hated Halie for it. "Listen, work's been crazy today. Think we could put it off another day?" The excuse rang hollow to his own ears, and he winced at the long silence on the line.

"You sure it's just work?" Her voice had gone from warm and sultry to cool and insecure. "Not…something else?"

Ben squeezed the keys and they bit into his palm. "It's just work." And that was true on one level, wasn't it?

What could he do? Tell Reese that Halie was blackmailing

him into seducing her? Make Reese doubt everything that had happened between them? He couldn't do that. When they were together, he couldn't have Reese thinking, on any level, that it had anything to do with Halie, her program, or the future of Hawk Construction. None of that mattered. He just wanted her. Plain and simple.

"Do you still want me to come over tonight?" she asked quietly.

Yes. "Come Monday," he said. He'd track Halie down at her office Monday morning, tell her what she could do with her little deal. Then he'd be free to be with Reese.

There would be other jobs. Other opportunities. Maybe not like this, but they'd be there. Eventually.

Silence stretched between them, long and tense. "What are you afraid of, Ben?"

"I'm not afraid. I care about you. I want to do this right."

"I care about you too," she said, her voice far away.

He slid to the floor, squeezing his eyes shut against the frustration and anger boiling inside him. He swallowed it down and it burned in his gut.

"Monday," she said softly.

"Monday."

She took a breath. "Listen, you know you can tell me if you've changed your mind. If you don't want this."

He flinched. "Reese." He couldn't blame her for doubting him. "Monday night, I'm going to get you naked. I'm going to make you come again, and this time when I do it, I'm going to be inside you."

She moaned softly. "Monday," she repeated.

Then he heard the click as she disconnected the call.

"Damn it!" He chucked the keys at the opposite wall. The clang echoed through the empty house as he buried his head in his hands.

CHAPTER EIGHTEEN

Reese stared at her phone and wondered for hundredth time that weekend if Ben would call. If he'd change his mind. She thought about sending him a text. Maybe a suggestive picture. She narrowly resisted the urge.

It was Saturday evening. She could go for a drink. She could watch a movie. Maybe Trish wanted company?

But she didn't want to do any of those things. She wanted Ben.

Monday, he'd said. But she didn't want to wait.

"I'm ready to take the life I want," she said softly. And as she found her keys, she knew Halie would be proud.

***

The first thing Ben heard when he walked in his front door Saturday night was the mechanical whir of his jetted tub. He closed his eyes against the ache the sound shot through him—everything he wanted and everything he couldn't have just beyond his bedroom doors.

She was here. In his tub. Relaxing or extending an invitation?

He unbuttoned his shirt and wandered toward the

bedroom. He had to stay away. He wouldn't let Halie use him in some power play. Even if Hawk Construction needed the job. Even if he wanted Reese more than anything.

Two steps into his bedroom and he froze. The bathroom door sat open, filling the room with the sounds of rushing water.

He'd promised, hadn't he? *"If you left the door open..."*

His hand trembled slightly as he reached the final buttons on his shirt. He took a step toward the bathroom, his feet moving of their own accord, then he forced himself to back up.

Water sloshed and he pictured her moving beneath the bubbles. Was she touching herself? Sliding her hands along slick skin? Teasing hard nipples with her fingers?

His cock pulsed hard at the image, and his hands itched to touch, to take.

At his side, his cell buzzed, someone calling.

He brought it to his ear, eyes never leaving the open door. "Hello."

"Ben?" Her voice was soft. "You're avoiding me."

He squeezed his eyes shut, swallowed hard. "I don't want to be."

"Prove it."

"What?"

More shifting water. "You want me?"

"Yes."

"Prove it."

He chucked his phone across the room.

Two steps and he was in the bathroom looking at her— flushed cheeks and shy smile, hair piled on top of her head in a loose ponytail. As soon as his eyes met hers, he knew he was done for.

Did it make any difference? He wasn't taking the contract. Being with Reese would have nothing to do with Halie.

"I'm not going to let you push me away," she said softly, her breasts rising from the bubbles with her deep inhalation.

"I wasn't trying to." God, she was gorgeous.

"No?" She trailed her hand over her collarbone, then parted the bubbles as it drifted between her breasts and into the water. Lower.

He let out a slow breath. "Reese…"

She rolled to her knees and leaned her elbows on the edge of the tub. "Come here."

He could turn away, but he knew he wouldn't. Pandora's box had been opened and he wanted what was inside.

He crossed to her. "We should talk."

"Mmm," she said, "yes, I definitely like it when we talk." Her fingers went to his waistband and popped the button, unzipped his fly. That task complete, she peeled his jeans and briefs down his hips in a single tug that left his cock exposed and jutting out hard and thick and inches from her lips.

"I never got to do this," she murmured, eyes flashing to his. "Reese…"

She leaned forward, laved the underside of his cock with her hot tongue.

Ben's breath left him in a rush. "Jesus."

She gave an impish grin and dragged her tongue along the length of him again—tasting him, wetting him, teasing him.

Cupping his balls in her hand, she opened her mouth and slid it over him. Just the head at first, with soft, teasing kisses that had him fisting his hands with need. Slowly, she opened, pulled him deeper, increased the pressure, the suction.

He slid his hands into her hair, not guiding her, not moving her, just wanting to touch her, to feel closer to her.

She moaned—a long, slow sound that vibrated against the sensitive head of his dick.

"Reese." He slid his hands into her hair now, wanting more, planning where he'd put his hands and his mouth.

She pulled back, then moved her mouth over him again, sucking him hard and taking him deep. The movement ripped a groan from his chest. He knotted his hands in her hair.

"God, that's good." He eased her back, struggled to even his breathing.

Swollen lips, flushed cheeks, dark eyes, she was a fucking

dream.

How had they gone so long without it coming to this? The tension between them had been a dance. Pulling them together. Pushing them apart. And she was right. He'd been afraid. He felt it now, making him want to bolt even as he wanted to take her in his arms.

"I want you, Ben."

Something ached in his chest at those words, as if only her saying them could make him realize how long he'd waited to hear them.

She stepped out of the tub, hitting the switch on the wall and silencing the jets. As she closed the space between them, his cock pressed into the soft flesh of her belly.

He *needed* to touch her, to give to her, to have her under his hands and mouth. He'd spent the last twenty-four hours avoiding the sinking feeling that Halie's visit had placed them on a precarious edge, that he could lose Reese at any moment.

He needed to wash away that fear with the taste of her.

"Is this..." He forced himself to ask the question. "Is this one of your steps?"

She stared at him for a moment. "Are you serious?" She turned and walked away. She was naked, wet, her round ass red from the heat of the tub, and she was walking away from him.

Fuck. He'd screwed this up.

He pulled up his jeans, zipping them before following her.

But when he stepped into his bedroom, she wasn't covering herself or sitting in the corner with crossed arms.

She was spread out on his bed, staring at the ceiling, her fingertips skating across her hipbones.

She pushed herself up on her elbows to look at him. "Does it matter? Do you need to tell yourself you're helping me? Do you need to believe this is part of the program?"

He sat next to her on the bed and skimmed his fingers across her collarbone, down between her breasts. At her shiver, he ran his fingers to her breast, cupped the weight of it in his hand. He lowered his mouth and flicked her nipple with his tongue before drawing it into his mouth.

She gasped. Moaned. "Tell yourself whatever you need, Ben. Just fuck me."

He met her eyes. *Just fuck me.* God, he wanted to. And he would. Consequences be damned, he couldn't walk away from her like this. Hot. Naked. Sweet. Begging. "I want the truth."

She swallowed, arched into his touch. "There's no step."

"Good," he growled.

"You're okay with that?"

"Hell yes." He let his gaze drift over her. "Spread your legs for me."

She parted her thighs obediently, exposing herself to him little by little.

"More," he commanded.

Again, she obeyed, and he ran his hands over her torso, down her sides, thumbs sweeping over her stomach and moving back to her breasts. She gasped at his touch, arching into it.

When he lowered his mouth to hers, he poured everything he had into the kiss. The fear, the hope, the years-caged potent longing.

She slid her hand into his open shirt and ran them over his abs, his chest. When she dipped them low again, her fingers slipped into his waistband and brushed the head of his dick.

He hissed. "God, Reese." He buried his face against her neck, taking in her scent—that floral smell of her soap and shampoo.

She wrapped her hand around his cock and stroked. "I can't tell you how many times I've thought about getting you in my hands."

The words whipped something wicked and hungry through him, and he sucked at her neck, his need nearly violent with its intensity.

Reese gasped. Ben held her steady as he moved down her body, reluctantly escaping her grasp, but needing to taste her. He sucked lightly at the skin at her waist, ran his tongue around her navel, scraped his teeth across one hipbone, the other.

When he pulled back to look, his heart was pounding.

He settled his hand between her legs. "Let me kiss you here."

At her sharp inhalation, he lowered his mouth to her parted legs, ran his tongue over the swollen lips of her sex, tasted her again for the first time in six years. He licked her, sucked at her hot slick folds of flesh until her hips rolled and her whimpers grew louder.

"Ben," she cried, her hands in his hair, her hips bucking against his mouth. "Please." She tugged at his hair, repeated, "Please."

He groaned. He needed hours—*days*—with her naked body, listening to her moan as he touched, kissed, sucked. But he couldn't deny that plea.

He shucked his pants and shirt while watching her. Her eyes dark with want, her dark hair splayed over the pillow. He kept his eyes on her as he searched for a condom in the nightstand.

Something hard and hot knotted in his chest, and he pushed back the irrational fear.

Her tongue darted out to wet her lips as he rolled the protection down his thick shaft.

He lowered himself carefully over her and settled between her thighs. "Tell me what you want, Reese."

"I want you, Ben. Inside me. Please." She lifted her hips, notching his cock against her slick heat.

He stared into her eyes as he slowly entered her.

His chest tightened with emotion. She was tight heat around his cock, and he gritted his teeth, forcing himself to take it slow, to give her body time to stretch.

Her nails dug into his shoulder blades and she brought up her knees. "Deeper."

With a ragged gasp, he obeyed, watching her face, listening to her soft moans as he filled her. And as he moved inside her, his hands framing her face, memorizing every flash of pleasure, he understood something. He knew why he'd been so damn scared. This wasn't just sex.

This was making love.

Pleasure coiled, tightened and spiraled, deeper and higher all at once. Sex had never felt like this. She curled her fingers into his back, fisted them in his hair.

When he felt her edging closer to orgasm, he put his mouth against her ear. "I love having my dick inside you. I love tasting you on my lips."

She gasped, bucking under him at his words. And as she came, he thought, *I love you*, but he didn't say it. Instead, he buried his face into her neck, lost himself in her scent, and followed her.

CHAPTER NINETEEN

Reese vaguely registered a shrill sound.

Ben kissed the crook of her neck. "Do you need to get that?"

Slowly, her brain resumed a few basic functions. Her cell. Ringing. "What's the number?"

Ben grabbed the phone off the nightstand. He raised a brow as he looked at the display. "My brother."

She took the phone and connected the call. "Hello?"

"Reese, are you okay?"

"I…I'm good." *Half naked with your brother.* "You?"

"Well, I was pretty good, and then I went to pick up my date. I think she's standing me up."

Ben was eyeing her.

Reese stood. She couldn't sit naked on the bed with Ben while she talked to his brother. She ran a hand through her hair. "I'm so sorry, Mark. I completely forgot."

"Need to cancel?"

Jaw hard, Ben pushed himself off the bed.

"Rain check?"

"Sure," Mark said. "Unless you still want to see that movie. I could come get you. Where are you?"

"I'm…" She looked at Ben. Telling Mark where she was

would just add insult to injury. "No, don't come. I'll make it up to you."

Ben's eyes flashed to hers, and she couldn't mistake what she saw there for anything other than the fury that it was. His jaw ticked.

"Tomorrow?"

Reese bit her lip. "Yeah, that could work." She met Ben's eyes. "I'm really sorry."

"I'll be honest. This is the first time I've ever been stood up for a fake date," Mark said. "I'll spend the evening tending to my tattered heart, but I should be okay by tomorrow."

She ended the call and squeezed her eyes shut. How had this even happened? She was just in one brother's bed and supposed to be on a date with another. She was completely head over heels in love with one brother, and the other loved her.

Love triangles were overrated.

When she opened her eyes, Ben sat at the edge of the bed, head in his hands, fingers threaded through his hair.

"So, you're probably wondering what that was all about."

He dropped his hands and glared up at her. "A date with *Mark*? Really? Is this what you two were so busy planning Thursday night?"

She flinched. "It's not like that," she said softly. "It's not a big deal. It's just one of my steps."

Ben pushed himself off the bed and paced the length of his bedroom. "Going out with Mark is one of your steps?"

"Sure, and it's No. Big. Deal."

He stopped pacing and looked at her. "Who are you? Because the Reese I knew wouldn't sit there telling a guy she just slept with that he should be okay with her going out with another...with his brother."

"I'm sorry. Did I miss something? Are we in some exclusive relationship now?"

"What? You need a ring on your finger to know I might be a little pissed about you going out with Mark?"

"I told you it's not like that. It's just a step. I'm faking my way through, remember?"

His jaw ticked. "Of course it is. God forbid you not complete one of Halie's Holy Steps."

"You, of all people, should appreciate those steps," she hissed.

"Me *of all people?*"

"Halie's the one who told me to have lunch with you the other day. She's the one who convinced me to keep an open mind about what could happen while I was with you. It was my step eight."

"Right. Because that's what all of this is for. Everything between us, everything that's changed in our relationship—it's all because of that goddamn program."

A chill snaked through her and she rubbed her arms. "I didn't realize it was such a hardship for you."

He looked at the ceiling. "Is this really the kind of girl you want to become, Reese? Screw one guy before you're out the door to slide into bed with his brother?"

Her breath left her in a rush and she staggered back. Her jaw tightened. "Fuck *you*, Ben. You don't get to control what I do with my body."

"Oh, right. That's Halie's job."

She crossed her arms. "You're being unreasonable. Even Mark knows it's a fake date. Just a step."

"As fake as all the steps you did with me?"

"Ben—"

"Come on, Reese. Anyone with eyes can see that you've had a crush on my brother. Doesn't it seem the slightest bit convenient that he's showing an interest *now?*"

She froze. Outside. Inside. Cold wrapped around her and she could hardly move her lips to speak. "What's that supposed to mean?"

"It means that Halie got to him. She told him to take you out, to flirt with you and make you feel good."

Another chill. Cold on top of cold. "Mark told you that?"

"No, but it's pretty damn likely. That's the way that woman functions. She came to me at the beginning of your program, asked me to 'help' you."

Something frozen in her gut felt like it was breaking in two. "She did?" God, it hadn't mattered that Halie had gone to Mark, but *Ben*?

"Then she wanted me to seduce you. Held the contract for the McCormack Manor job over my head. Makes sense that she got to Mark too. She was playing us against each other to make you feel good about yourself."

She drew in a breath but her lungs wouldn't take it. The air wouldn't go in. "You did this because Halie *told* you to?"

Ben flinched. "Shit. I didn't mean—"

"You're such a hypocrite."

He took a breath. "No. I wasn't going to take the contract. I'm not going to. I gave that up. For you. But you're going out with *Mark*? He hardly knew you existed before your makeover, but he's the stud, right? He's the real prize."

"Are you serious?" Oh, God, that chasm in her stomach. It could just swallow her whole.

He pulled a hand through his hair. "You expect me sit back and pretend this is okay?"

The pain in her gut was spinning, a growing vortex that was beginning to scream in her ears. "How many years have we been friends, Ben? How many opportunities did you have?" She shook her head. "I wanted you and you knocked me down. You say Mark didn't notice me until after the makeover, but I think you have it backwards. *You* didn't want me before. You rejected the quiet, lonely caterpillar. You wanted Halie's butterfly."

"You have no idea how long I've wanted you."

"You're right. I don't. But Mark? He wanted me five years ago, long before the makeover."

"Five years ago?" He grunted. "Is that what he told you?"

"He didn't have to tell me," she said softly, her stomach pitching. She was going to be sick.

"What do you mean he…" Ben seemed to suddenly register her meaning and his eyes locked on hers. "No."

"Five years ago. You said you didn't want me. You told me

not to ask you for more."

His face contorted. "Reese?"

"I needed someone, and Mark was there. *He* wanted me." She dropped her voice. "Still does."

His eyes blazed, and she recognized the anger, the hurt. "Then go, Reese. Mark wants you? You want him? No one's standing in your way."

She shook her head. "I chose *you*, you asshole."

"Really? You *chose me*? Was that before or after you fucked my brother?"

Part of her registered the pain on his face, part of her mind understood he was hurt, that these were words he'd regret later. But she had to put those parts aside and focus her energy on surviving, on clawing her way to safety and away from the icy vortex spinning wildly as it ripped her heart from her chest.

"Bye, Ben."

***

Reese squeezed a pillow against her stomach and swallowed back the tears she'd been fighting since she left Ben's house. God, why did it have to hurt so much?

She wanted to believe this was a bump, a little argument they'd move past, but the dread in her stomach felt so familiar and her red dress hung on the back of her bedroom door, reminding her of her old foolish assumptions, reminding her of the last time she'd dressed just for him and put her heart on the line.

After he'd found out about his girlfriend dying, Reese had been there for him, been a friend. That's what he'd needed, and she couldn't imagine anything else. He'd been a mess, and she'd been there, never questioning their relationship or his intentions. Being his friend hadn't been a decision, just the natural response to his tragedy. But as months came and went, she realized that she was no longer the almost-girlfriend. Graduation had come and gone and she'd passed up a good job offer back in Kentucky and accepted a permanent position with WJRK. She waited out the anniversary of Lisa's death, waited out the long summer after.

Then Ben had asked her to join him for a fancy dinner with the local homebuilders, and she thought their holding pattern had finally come to an end.

Wearing a little black dress and her mom's pearls, she'd waited for Ben to pull her close during a dance, to brush his lips over her neck, to reroute their relationship to its original course.

Before she knew it, the evening had ended and they were sitting in his truck, nothing changed between them but her expectations.

"Thanks for coming tonight," he said with a grin. "I hate this part as much as my dad does, but unlike him I understand rubbing elbows is necessary if you want to stay alive in this business."

"I liked going," she said softly, clutching her purse in her lap. "I don't remember the last time I had an excuse to dress up."

"You clean up nice." He reached for the radio and winked at her, sending a little shiver of anticipation up her spine.

"Ben?" She swallowed down her terror and forced herself to ask the question that had been haunting her for months. "Are you ever going to kiss me again?"

His fingers froze at the radio dial.

A car alarm sounded down the street. A dog barked and someone shouted.

Suddenly, the closed car didn't have enough air. Reese's cheeks burned and her skin was tight and hot.

Ben dropped his hand from the tuner and he squeezed it into a fist at his side. He turned to look out the window, away from her. "I thought we were friends."

Her eyes slammed shut, her heart plummeting. "We are."

"Don't ask me for more." His voice was so low she almost couldn't hear him. "I can't."

"So, we're just supposed to go on pretending that our night together never happened?" God, why was she still here? Was she really so pathetic? Begging for an explanation?

When he turned to her, the pain in his eyes revealed how fresh a year-old wound could be. "I regret everything about that night, and I would take it all back if I could."

And that really said it all, didn't it? The most passionate, intense night of her life, and he'd regretted every minute of it.

She flinched and reached for her door handle. "Goodnight, Ben." She stumbled from the car and toward her apartment. She didn't cry. Couldn't—not when her tears would be as much for him as for herself. She understood, and yet that didn't keep the shattered pieces of her heart from tearing her insides to shreds.

A week later, she'd found herself drinking a beer next to Mark. Luke had just opened his new bar and they were all making a habit of supporting his venture.

"So, are you and my brother ever going to get together?" Mark had asked.

"I can honestly say we are not." She did her best to sound like she didn't care. Maybe she pulled it off. "I'm the type of girl whose friendship guys value, blah, blah, blah."

Mark grunted. "I don't."

"What?"

He shrugged. "I don't value your friendship." His eyes dropped to her mouth. "I'll prove how little I value it, if you'll let me."

She'd needed that, needed that moment. They'd laughed, and the next morning, she'd woken up in his bed in a panic. Because, want to or not, she still loved Ben.

She made her walk of shame back to her apartment and found Ben there with a bottle of wine and a handful of skeeball tokens. She'd recognized it as a peace offering, and she'd accepted. Because she missed him. Because she told herself she didn't need more from him. And because, though she wouldn't admit it to a soul and denied it when Trish or Masey dared suggest it, she believed it was only a matter of time before Ben made his move.

A couple more years passed and she found Lance flirting

with her, buying her a drink, and asking her how much longer she was going to let "that carpenter guy" lead her on.

How many times was she going to let Ben break her heart?

Reese squeezed her pillow tighter and buried her face in it. When her phone buzzed, a look at the display told her Mark was calling.

CHAPTER TWENTY

Ben was two and a half beers into what he intended to be a most-excellent drunk when Mark walked into the PitStop.

Cries of "Hawk! Hawk!" filled Ben's ears and made him want to hit someone. Preferably a tall, dark, and famous someone who shared a bunch of Ben's DNA.

"How's Chicago's biggest asshole?" Ben called, a little too loudly. "Thought you had a date tonight. Or maybe you're done with her now and here to spit in my beer." He pushed his glass across the table toward his brother. "Or was there something else of mine you wanted to ruin?"

Too late, he saw Reese behind Mark, then registered the pain on her face. *Shit.*

Slowly, she pushed Mark aside and approached Ben's booth, her dark eyes shimmering. Anger? Tears? Both?

They stared at each other, and Ben could hear his heart pounding in his ears. Funny it could still do that—beat—when for the last two hours it had felt like nothing but a mass of concrete weighing down his chest.

"I waited for you," she said softly. "Months, I waited. And then you told me you didn't want me."

"I wanted you." He took in a shaky breath, shot a glare at Mark. "Everyone knew that. Mark knew that."

"You wanted me? Is that why you told me you wouldn't be more than my friend?"

"I was terrified, Reese." He reached for her, but she stepped back. "I didn't want to lose you."

She nodded. "Yeah, and that was your choice. Fine. And I slept with Mark. Probably stupid, since I was still in love with you…"

Ben drew in a shaky breath. She'd been in love with him.

"…But it was my choice," she continued. "I wasn't *yours*. You. Didn't. Want. Me. You didn't want me until I changed my clothes and hair. You didn't want me until I looked like this. Mark? He wanted me from the beginning. Just as I am."

Behind her, Mark dropped his head, studied the floor.

Ben swallowed.

"So don't talk about me like I did you wrong, Ben. Don't talk about me like I was stolen from you."

"I didn't expect you to run to my brother," he said, trying to explain, trying to get her to see how much he hurt.

"But I did. Because I needed to be wanted and *he* wanted me. I'm not some *toy* that someone *ruined* before you could get a chance to play. I made mistakes. Not telling you about what happened with Mark? That was a mistake. But you made mistakes too."

"What did you want from me?" He slammed his palm against the table. "Every time I looked at you, I felt guilty. For wanting you when I was supposed to be grieving. For wanting you when I was with Lisa and you were just this cute girl at the bar. I felt guilty for what I'd been doing while *she* was dying."

Sympathy softened her features and he hated it, wished she'd look angry again.

"I didn't want to lose you too," he said.

"I know." She stepped back. "All I wanted was for you to be brave enough to try. I know you were scared, and I wanted to be worth the risk." She took another step.

"Reese—" But he was talking to her back because she was on her way out the door. Leaving him. Again.

Fuck.

Ben closed his eyes and when he opened them again Mark sat in the booth across from him.

"Fuck off," Ben muttered, but his heart wasn't in it, and Mark didn't take the bait, just signaled the waitress for a beer.

They were quiet a long time, studying their beers instead of facing each other.

"Why Reese?" Ben asked finally. "Dad, the company, whatever, I can deal. But Reese?" He made a fist, as if that could release the ache in his chest.

"You're not the only one who loves her," Mark said softly.

Ben looked up, and the ache intensified because the truth was in Mark's eyes.

"You know why I first fell for her?"

Ben looked away. He didn't need to hear this. He, of all people, understood falling for Reese Regan, understood wanting her even when he set his mind against it.

"I wanted someone to look at me the way she looks at you."

Ben grunted. "Are you kidding me? Women crawl out of the woodwork for you."

Mark lifted a shoulder. "They want The Hawk. They want someone who will flirt with them, someone who will push the boundaries and make them blush. Some of them even want sex. But they don't want me. They sure as hell don't respect me."

"I didn't realize you wanted *respect*."

"When Reese looks at you, her whole body goes soft. Like she's found happiness. Like she's come home and never wants to leave again. No woman has ever looked at me like that. I wanted what you had, and I fell for her. And I'm sorry as hell about that because I didn't want to fall for your girl. But I did anyway. And damn it, Ben. How long was I supposed to watch you lead her on and turn her down? I waited. You told her you didn't want more, and I made my move."

"And this time?" Ben said, his voice gruff.

"I asked you at Dad's retirement. You said you were just friends and I believed you. I wanted to believe you, but when I saw you all over her on Thursday night, I let it go. Do you have any idea how hard that is? Just bowing out to my little brother? And then you act like a fucking undeserving dick."

"I didn't want to lose her," Ben heard himself say again. He was staring at the door like an idiot. As if she might come back through and throw herself in his arms. "I was so scared to lose her."

"But you did."

***

When Lance had left Reese, she'd taken a week of vacation from work and had spent the entire seven days sitting on her couch in her bathrobe, watching sad movies. She'd cried and grieved—for what they'd once had and for what she'd only hoped they might have. Trish and Masey took turns checking on her, bringing her therapeutic ice cream and listening to her rant about the man who'd broken her heart.

She'd been with Lance for three years, and it had hurt when he left. Her pride and her heart were wounded, but with some tending she'd been able to return to life, return to normal.

After her week-long ice cream binge, she'd called Ben and asked to meet him at the PitStop. They'd done shots together, shared a few choice words about Lance, and it was almost like her time with Lance had never happened.

Her fight with Ben hadn't left her like that. She didn't feel angry. She didn't want to call her friends and rant and rave over how he'd done her wrong. She didn't want to talk about it at all. She felt empty. Her heart hadn't been broken, it'd been ripped from her chest and taken hostage.

So she'd poured herself into her work—easy to do with the masquerade ball approaching this weekend. She hadn't let herself grieve or scream. And when her cell rang and the screen told her it was Ben on the line, she hadn't answered. She already knew what he'd say, how he'd propose they resolve their problems, and she didn't want to hear it.

Now, in her office, two weeks after he'd taken her heart

hostage, it was no different. She hit the button on the side of her phone to send the call to voicemail, though she knew he wouldn't leave one.

She wouldn't avoid him forever. Eventually, she'd take the call, she'd listen to him suggest they go back to being friends. Eventually, she'd decide how she was going to respond to that suggestion.

But not until after this weekend. She couldn't afford to break down before she made it through Saturday night.

"You've been quiet this week."

Reese snapped her head up to see Halie standing in the doorway. She'd deliberately avoided the woman.

She was angry at Halie's presumptiveness, yes, but Reese couldn't make herself regret the changes she'd made in the last months.

She loved her job, loved being the new Reese—a woman who made people listen and take note, not just a wallflower so easily ignored and forgotten.

But that didn't excuse Halie's actions.

Reese crossed her arms on her desk. "I thought we would wait to talk until after the masquerade ball."

Halie frowned. "That doesn't sound good."

Reese shrugged. "I don't think anything I have to say will come as a surprise to you."

"I called Ben this morning," Halie said. "Tried to get him to reconsider about the Manor remodel."

"How'd that go?"

"I don't think he'd complain if tomorrow's news held a report of my body being recovered from Lake Michigan, but he's not ready to commit the act himself just yet."

Not a bad analogy, considering the magnitude of her crimes. "Do you always handle your clients this way? Asking the men in their lives to get involved—bribing them to take the women on dates, to have sex with them?"

Halie's cheeks flushed a dark pink. Reese hadn't ever seen her flush. "Sometimes. More lately. I might have let my own relationship problems escalate my need to assist others' relationships."

"And by *assist* you mean *control?*"

She gave a sad smile and toyed with the pearls at her neck. "It's been brought to my attention that I might have some control issues."

For the first time, Reese noticed the woman's large engagement ring was gone. "Your fiancé left you?"

"I left him." She seemed to realize she was fidgeting and dropped her hand to her side. "It was time."

"I'm sorry."

Halie waved away Reese's words. "It's over. You were asking about how I usually run my business, and I want to have this conversation. I want to hear your thoughts—your honest feedback."

Reese leaned back in her chair. "No, I'd rather you still be speaking to me at the event this weekend."

The woman's shoulders dropped. "That bad?"

"No. Not all bad." Reese pushed herself up from her chair. "Look at the results."

Halie shrugged. "I do know where to shop."

"It's not just the clothes, Halie. It's me. I really, truly feel better about myself than I have in…" She trailed off, trying to remember a time she'd possessed the confidence she did now. "Never. I've never felt this good."

"But?"

Reese walked around her desk and perched on the front of it, choosing her words carefully. "But I think your program is two things at once. Half of it is this wonderful, progressive look at women's identities and self-esteem that allows them to really examine what they want for themselves and go after it in a way that is both healthy and ambitious."

"That sounds good," Halie said cautiously.

"It is!" Reese said. "If it were that alone, I'd send my *niece* to you. You know, once she's forty or so."

"But the other half?"

Reese shook her head and crossed her arms. "The other half is this tired cliché, helping women find their worth through the eyes of men." She shrugged. "I'm not saying it can't be about feeling sexy. I'm not saying there's anything wrong with finding pleasure in being desirable. I understand all that. But if women can't leave it feeling good about themselves without you bribing men to flirt with them, woo them, *sleep* with them? Well, if that's the case, it's not much of a program at all, is it?"

Halie took a step back, her eyes wide. "I guess you told me," she said, and Reese could practically see her walls going up.

"That's just it, Halie. I don't think your program needs it. You've built something amazing, but your own lack of faith is corrupting it."

Reese's phone beeped on her desk, a meeting reminder. She grabbed her purse. "I have to go down to the venue to check on everything before tomorrow night."

Halie gave a sharp nod. "That's what I pay you for."

Reese sighed. "It's okay if you're angry with me, but think about it." She squeezed Halie's arm, hoping the woman could see the irony in the situation. If Sex Goddess 101 didn't work, Reese would have never had the courage to criticize it.

***

Ben had never hit a woman, had never wanted to, but when Halie McCormack pulled onto his job site on Friday night, he found his hands balling into fists.

"Good to see you," she called.

"I don't remember extending an invitation." Yes, he was being an ass, but this was the woman who had pitted two brothers against each other in the name of her program. She'd taken the sexiest woman he knew and destroyed his relationship with her to "make her sexy." Yeah, he was being an ass, but he figured he'd earned the right.

"Want to tell me when you're going to get started on the Manor?"

"I don't want the job," Ben said, his voice low. "Not at any price."

Halie tucked a lock of hair behind her ear. "Mr. Hawk, if looks could kill, I'm pretty sure they'd be making arrangements for my funeral."

"If you want Hawk Construction to do the job, you're going to have to go through my brother."

"Not interested," Mark's voice came behind him.

Ben turned, surprised. Mark had been working the Granger job all week, but in the old days when Mark took time away from his post as "The Hawk" to play business owner, he'd been the last in and the first out, taking any excuse to get out of work. This week, Mark had put in longer hours than Ben every day. It was a change Ben hadn't adjusted to yet.

"We're not just about money," Mark said, tucking his hands in his pockets. "It matters to us how people do business."

Ben locked eyes with Mark. They hadn't spoken much this week. What was there to say? They loved the same girl. But here Mark was, getting Ben's back.

Ben nodded to his brother. As peace offerings went, it wasn't very flashy, but he knew Mark saw it for what it was.

"I'm not the evil person you're making me out to be," Halie said.

"You screw with people's lives." Ben turned back to her, ready to battle.

Her shoulders dropped. "I get people to acknowledge what they want. Sometimes they don't even know, but I try to help them figure it out. Reese didn't know she wanted you. She wasn't ready to admit it."

"Right. And to figure out what they want, women need men? They need lingerie shopping and phone sex? They need brothers fighting over them? Isn't that all a little anti-feminist?"

Halie sighed. "You can save yourself the lecture. Reese beat you to it."

That warmed him a little. *Good girl.*

Then Halie shocked him by laughing.

Mark was staring at him, brow raised. "Phone sex?"

"I don't know about the phone sex," Halie said. "But I

don't think you're grasping the significance of that date with Mark. Don't you wonder why she didn't just go on a date with *you?*"

Only a few hundred times. Ben lifted a shoulder.

"The step was to go on a date with a man she would never marry." Halie looked at Mark and winced. "Sorry."

"What?" Ben turned to Mark.

Mark shrugged. "Reese told me that. I was just a means to an end."

"Shit." Ben ran a hand through his hair. "This is such a mess."

Halie narrowed her eyes. "Did she tell you phone sex was one of her steps?"

Ben crossed his arms. "Yes. She said—" He dropped his arms. *Fuck.* "She asked what I would do if phone sex was her next step."

Mark grunted. "I guess you gave her your answer, didn't you?"

Ben tilted his head back and looked at the gray October sky. He missed her so damn much. Two weeks and she wasn't taking his calls. Not that he could blame her.

Reese had been right. He'd been afraid. Terrified. He hadn't been enough for Lisa, his first love, his first heartbreak. And the idea of Reese sleeping with Mark had sent that old terror through him. Not being enough. Not measuring up.

"Are you going to win her back or not?" Halie asked.

"She won't take my calls," Ben grumbled. Damn. He sounded like a whiny little shit.

Mark was looking at him, that expectant eyebrow raised.

"Maybe I can help," Halie said.

Ben glared at her. "You've helped enough."

"Just hear me out?"

And because he had no better ideas aside from staging a sit-in protest at Reese's condo, he listened.

By the end of the conversation, Mark was grinning and Ben was feeling something in his chest he thought might have been hope. The feeling scared him enough that his fingers shook slightly as he sent the text to Reese.

I won't be able to be in your auction on Saturday. I'll get Luke to come in my place.

CHAPTER TWENTY-ONE

Ben scratched a few more notes about McCormack Manor as he made a final tour. His crew would start work here as soon as they finished the Granger job.

"She's a beauty," someone said from behind him.

Ben turned around to see his father standing in the old mansion's musty ballroom, Mark behind him.

"Dad? What are you doing here?"

His dad shoved his hands in his pockets, his shoulders hunching slightly. He seemed smaller somehow, as if he'd suddenly aged fifteen years. Had Ben just not been paying attention?

"Mark brought me," his father said, his voice creaking like the wooden hallways of the Manor. "He thought I should see the kind of job you've been getting Hawk Construction."

Ben looked to Mark.

Mark pointed his thumb to the front of the house. "I'm going to wait out front."

Something tightened in Ben's chest as his brother winked at him then turned to go.

"I don't want you to give you the wrong impression, Dad," Ben said when Mark was gone. "This may be the only job like this we ever get."

His dad nodded. "Yeah, but you're going for 'er. You've got that in you. Not afraid to try for something better." He rocked back on his heels. "Me? I was always too scared to lose what I had to go after something better."

Ben's throat grew thick and he thought of Reese, thought of how he'd lost her to Lance, thought of what might have been if he'd given her more of himself five years ago. "I get scared too," he said. "I like to think it's never too late to try for something better."

Was that his voice? It sounded small and vulnerable. Like he was a little boy again, trying to get his father's attention over his louder, bigger, more boisterous older brother.

The old man looked to the picture window that looked out into the gardens. "I'm proud of you," he said, the words sounding awkward off his dried lips. "You might think Mark's the favorite, but I love you both. That boy just needs help finding himself. Always been a little lost. A little too worried about fitting in to make the best choices. You? You've always had it figured out. Always had your priorities straight."

Thaddeus Hawk wasn't the type of father who'd taught his boys it was okay to cry, so Ben didn't let himself speak. Instead, he took four steps and pulled the man into a hug.

His dad patted his back. One pat. Two. Three—the sign of true accomplishment. "Enough of that now."

Ben pulled back. "Can you imagine what we could do here?"

"Sure can." He looked at Ben expectantly, then, "You gonna tell me your plans or not?"

Ben grinned. "Let me show you around."

***

Mark looked at the gorgeous brunette in his arms and felt all the old emotions Reese's face inspired—the softness, the hope, the love, the guilt. "Thanks for the dance," he said hoarsely.

"Well, we better keep it short or face the wrath of that line of women here to get their hands on The Hawk." She smiled, but even through her feathered mask, he saw the sadness in her eyes.

"The place looks amazing," he said, pulling her closer. The masquerade ball was packed with Sex Goddess 101 graduates and hopefuls, their dates, and the men hoping to be their dates. The night had just begun, but by all accounts it was already a success.

"Thanks," she said. "I almost can't believe we pulled it off."

"Think Ben will show up?"

She lifted her shoulder. "He bailed on the auction, so he better not show his face." She was silent for a minute, then said, "Can you tell me something?"

"I can try."

"Why were you interested in me? Before the makeover, I mean? All those years ago."

The question took Mark by surprise.

"Was it just a rivalry thing between you and Ben?"

Mark stopped dancing and looked down at her. "You want a drink?"

"That would be good."

Mark led the way to the bar and ordered a whiskey for himself and a glass of red for Reese. "I'm a total fraud," he admitted, handing the glass to her.

"What are you talking about?"

He lifted a shoulder. "The Hawk. I pretty much hate that asshole."

She relaxed a little. "He is kind of a chauvinist."

"Kind of? He's a selfish bastard."

Now she smiled for real. "Maybe a little, but it's just a persona. That's not who you really are. The Hawk's an ass, sure. But Mark? He's a good guy."

He studied the amber liquid in his glass. "Maybe I'm a little bit of both. The guy who slept with you even though he knew you had a thing for his brother? Even though he knew his brother had a thing for you? That was the asshole."

"Don't." She set her wine on the counter and rubbed her bare arms. "It was a long time ago, and Ben had no *thing* for me. He made it painfully clear that he wasn't interested."

"Reese, if he hadn't been in love with you back then, he would have slept with you."

She wrinkled her brow, looking thoroughly unimpressed by his assessment. "Want to try another one?"

"I wish I had handled it differently, but I didn't. The guy who still likes you after all that time? The guy who just wants you both to be happy, despite that jealousy clawing his chest? That's the man I want to be, and I'm telling you now, my brother's an idiot, but he's only an idiot because you're the most important thing in his world."

She looked away, her eyes moist. "This sucks. It just does."

"Yeah," Mark said. "Agreed."

"Reese!"

Mark and Reese both turned to see Halie McCormack, all long legs and sparkle in her glittery silver dress and mask.

"Reese, it's time for step ten," Halie said, a grin stretching across her face.

"You're hilarious, Halie, but as impressive as I am at multitasking, I won't be completing step ten in the middle of an event." Reese frowned and shook her head. "And besides, I never completed step six and you never gave me a step nine."

"My steps don't work like that. You're ready."

Reese looked at the stage. "It's almost time for the bachelor and bachelorette auction."

Halie pulled her mask away from her eyes. "Exactly."

***

Reese stood at the back of the stage, her stomach flipping as their master of ceremonies auctioned off the first bachelor.

"I can't believe I'm doing this," Luke grumbled next to her.

"Buck up, soldier," Mark said. "It's for a good cause."

"Easy for you to say," Luke whined. "You haven't had that old lady making eyes at you all night."

"What old lady?" Reese asked, desperate for Luke's story to soothe her nerves.

"That old lady from the Senior Center? Proudly touts herself the first senior citizen Sex Goddess?"

"Mrs. Wisenowitz?" Reese said with a shriek.

"Ladies," the emcee announced, "our next bachelor is a Chi-town native and the owner of the PitStop Bar and Grill."

"Shake it, boyfriend," Reese commanded.

On cue, Luke pulled on his mask and stepped onto the stage.

"Can we start the bids at fifty dollars?"

"Seventy-five," Mrs. Wisenowitz called, pushing her walker toward the stage.

Luke strutted down their makeshift catwalk, shimmying his tux jacket off his shoulders.

The women in the audience screeched in response, followed by rapid-fire "One hundred," "One-fifty," "Three-seventy-five."

"Five hundred dollars," Mrs. Wisenowitz called.

Luke cast a desperate look over his shoulder, and Reese lifted her palms helplessly. Almost Home needed the money, he could suffer through one night as Mrs. W's boy toy.

"Sold for five hundred dollars to the beautiful young woman in the powder blue suit," the emcee said, ushering Luke off the stage.

Luke kissed Mrs. W on the cheek and the crowd applauded.

Reese turned to Mark. "Think you can match that?"

Mark waved a hand. "Easy."

"Good luck," she said softly.

"Maybe I'll meet the woman who can help me mend my broken heart."

"Give a warm welcome to *The Hawk*," the emcee was saying.

As Mark strutted to center stage, the crowd cheered. The bids started before the emcee could ask.

Reese was trying to calm herself by counting her breaths when she heard a woman's voice call over the crowd's cheers, "One thousand dollars."

Was that Masey? Bidding on Mark?

Reese swung around and, sure enough, Masey stood near the front of the stage in a hot pink poodle skirt and pink sequined mask, looking voluptuous and glamorous. And determined.

"Sold to the blond beauty for one thousand dollars!"

Masey crooked her finger at Mark, who looked a little perplexed as he joined her.

"Now, onto our first bachelorette," the emcee said, and Reese tried to breathe.

Very often people were surprised to learn that, though she could create a damn good spotlight, she hated to be in it. As she stepped onto the stage, hands shaking, butterflies rioting in her stomach, she realized that all the Sex Goddess lessons in the world weren't going to change that about her.

"Sex Goddess Inc.'s very own Reese Regan is a proud graduate of both the University of Chicago and Sex Goddess 101."

The odd juxtaposition made her pause a bit. If her classmates could see her now...

"Can we start bids at fifty dollars?"

She forced herself to take another step and another. The spotlight blinded her, and she couldn't see the audience. The silence probably only lasted seconds, but seemed to stretch out for minutes until someone called the first bid.

For the first time, she wondered who would buy her company for the night. When Halie had told her to auction herself, she'd been so wrapped up in her fear of being on the stage that her brain hadn't made it to what would happen after that.

Bids were to two hundred dollars now.

"Can I get two-fifty for this gorgeous lady in red?" the emcee asked.

Reese made an awkward little turn, trying to hide that she hated every second of this.

"How about free labor for the construction of Almost Home's new wing?"

She froze and looked out into the crowd. She couldn't see a

thing with the light glaring in her eyes.

"You've got yourself a bachelorette, sir," the emcee said. He took Reese's hand and led her to the stairs.

She shook with each step. Not nerves now but something else, something more.

The winning bidder was dressed in black with a black mask. He was broad shouldered and had shaggy blond hair, and Reese wanted to throw herself in his strong arms.

"Thank you for your generous donation."

"To have you, I would have given more," Ben said, taking her trembling hand.

"I would have been yours for less."

CHAPTER TWENTY-TWO

Ben held Reese close as the auctions wrapped up. She didn't look at him or touch him, but he kept his arm around her waist, afraid she might run off and he wouldn't get another chance.

She had to feel good about what this event—her event—had done for the women's shelter. He was so damn proud of her.

As soon as the band started playing, he led her to the dance floor. He pulled her as close as possible, a hand grazing her bare back. The music hummed, slow and sultry, while he searched her face.

"You came," she said, linking her arms around his neck and pressing her body against his.

The gentle sway of her hips had him remembering how she'd moved against his hand when he'd had her on that countertop, reminded of the way she'd moved under him on his bed.

God, she felt good in his arms.

"When we fought, you said I never wanted you before your makeover." He rubbed a thumb over the last spot of exposed skin at the base of her back. "Do you really believe that?"

"I don't know what I believe," she whispered, but her voice

hitched slightly.

He ran lazy fingertips up her spine and pressed his lips against the exposed length of neck.

"What are you doing?" But even as she asked, she tilted her head to give him better access.

He opened his mouth against her skin, smelling her, tasting her. She released a soft moan.

"You're so beautiful." He drew back. "This dress is begging to be peeled off you, but you know what really made me crazy?"

"Ben..." She pulled away, but he held her fast.

"You know those black pants you wear when we work out?"

She raised a brow. "My yoga pants?"

"The ones that fit your ass like a glove?" He groaned. "I've had more than one fantasy about peeling those off you. And that ugly brown robe? Do you have any idea how many times I've had to shove my hands in my pockets to keep from tugging it open? You walked around in it like it was supposed to have no effect on me."

She smiled slightly and leaned her head against his shoulder.

"God, Reese, I've always wanted you." Ben kept her body pressed close as they toured the dance floor. "Were you not there the day we met?"

She tensed in his arms. "You told me you regretted everything about that day."

He squeezed her more tightly. "I was an idiot."

They danced, and he kept his hand on her back. His mouth teased the edges of her ear until he couldn't handle it anymore, until he needed her alone.

He pulled her into a coatroom tucked behind a server station and shut the door behind them.

The door muffled the sounds from the dance floor, but he still spoke against her ear. "I loved every minute of touching you that night. You were sweet and sexy and so goddamn wet from the slightest touch."

He slipped a hand between their bodies. The satin slid

under his fingers as he touched her. At her soft moan, he cupped a breast in his hand, his thumb finding her taut nipple through the fabric. "I've never forgotten what you looked like, laid out on the couch for me, letting me open your legs and touch you."

He scraped her nipple with his thumb, and she moaned on a ragged breath. "You let me kiss you. Taste you. I've never forgotten how you tasted. Hot and wet against my mouth."

"I can't do this anymore."

"Do what?" The words came out hard and rough, but that was how he felt. Hard and rough and so fucking vulnerable it made him crazy.

"I can't pretend I'm okay with this flirting and teasing never going anywhere. I can't pretend the sex doesn't mean anything to me. I can't go back to the way things were before."

Laughter burst out of him at that. "*Before*? What before?"

"Before the kiss. Before the phone sex and…everything else."

He pressed her against the wall and slid his hands up her sides. "Before you started this program? When I wanted you every day and had to watch you moon over Mark?"

"He was safe. But you—"

He silenced her with a kiss, then slipped his hand into the slit of her skirt and dug his fingers into the bare flesh of her hip. "Or before that? When you moved in with Lance and dropped me from your life completely?" His fingers found the string above her hipbone and followed it to the small of her back.

She gasped and rocked her hips toward him.

He dropped his mouth to her ear. "Or should we go back to before that—to the day I walked you home for the first time, to the night you let me kiss you. You let me touch you." He circled his fingers at the small of her back, then let them dip, following the satin of her thong and tracing the seam of her ass.

Her breathing hitched and she drew in a shaky breath.

"I could go for that *before*. Before I had to pretend not to notice the way your hair curls when it's humid out, before I had to pretend I don't respond like any man would to the way your ass fills your jeans. Before I was so damn terrified I might screw up and lose you."

"Ben." She put her hands to his chest—to pull him close or push him away, he couldn't tell, but she did neither.

"Jesus, Reese, I can't go back to *before* either."

"I loved you," she said softly. "I was scared too."

"*Loved?*" he growled. "It's not past tense for me. Don't you know that? I fell in love with you six years ago, and I never stopped."

"Me either."

He pressed her against the wall. With one hand, he cuffed her hands above her head while the other curved into the flesh of her ass.

He lowered his mouth, slanted over her, and rubbed tongue against tongue. She moaned, sending a shudder through him.

He broke the kiss to remove their masks. He tried to memorize her like this—face flushed with desire, eyes clouded with want, lips swollen from his assault on her mouth. He traced the seam of her ass again, watching her lips part, her eyes go wide.

"You're so damn hot."

"We should go back to the party," she said, her breathing shallow.

"Definitely." He lifted her leg to his waist, opening her. "They'll be looking for you," he said, his fingers already sliding beneath the satin of her panties. He dipped his fingers into her, wetting them before tracing back up.

"God."

"Or you could stay in here with me," he whispered.

"Keep talking."

"You want me to talk or do something else with my mouth?"

She trembled against him, hands fumbling at his waistband. She released his cock from his pants and stroked.

"Reese," he groaned against her neck. God, her hands on

him were amazing.

"Please tell me you have a condom."

His cock pulsed harder, thicker. He almost suggested that they wait, that he take her home, but he saw it in her eyes. The heat, the need.

Ben took the package from his pocket and slid the condom on. "Hold on," he said, nodding to the coat rack.

She looked him in the eye and wrapped her hands around the metal bars over her head. "Do this before?"

"About a thousand times in my dreams." He pressed her into the wall and slid his hands behind her ass. "And it was always you in my arms."

She wrapped her legs around him, and he slowly slid inside her.

The cacophony of the party sounded on the other side of the door as they moved together.

She gasped as he filled her, breath catching as he pressed himself closer, deeper, held her, fucked her, loved her.

"Ben," she breathed.

She rolled her hips, rocked them. And he held her, slid inside her again and again.

"You're so amazing," he whispered. "I love you." He wanted to keep saying it, to keep kissing her, to stay inside her and never lose her again.

CHAPTER TWENTY-THREE

"Welcome!" Reese said, wrapping her arms around Tricia. "Sledgehammers are to the left, the bar is to the right!"

Halie was having a "Smash and Get Smashed" party at McCormack Manor to celebrate the beginning of the renovations. She'd invited half the town and insisted her employees invite their friends as well. Since Reese wasn't so sure about a bunch of intoxicated adults wielding sledgehammers, she was encouraging any wall smashing to happen early in the evening—before she and Ben hid the hammers.

Trish gave Reese a hug. "Don't you look cute in your little black dress? Really, could you please wear something dowdy so that boyfriend of your will keep his hands off you for a few minutes?"

"I know," Masey said, coming in behind Tricia. "Their sex life has given mine an inferiority complex."

Reese released Tricia and shrugged. "I could wear a brown bag on my head, and I'm pretty sure it wouldn't make a difference." She couldn't help but smile. Because it was true. Because Ben made her feel so damn sexy no matter what she was wearing. But mostly she smiled because she'd hardly stopped smiling in the last two months. She hadn't sold her condo, and yet somehow she found herself falling asleep next to Ben every night and waking up next to him every morning.

"Mark's over by the bar," Ben said, joining them by the front doors. "He was asking for you, Masey."

"Which way was the bar again?" Masey asked.

Ben pointed.

"Okay, see you later," Masey said, turning in the opposite direction.

Ben frowned. "What's that about?"

"She's been acting weird since she bought him as her escort at the masquerade ball," Reese said, frowning after her friend.

"Think they did it?" Tricia asked.

Ben grunted. "Let's hope so. Mark needs a new woman to pursue."

Reese nudged him.

"Mark and Masey?" Tricia said. "Damn, can you imagine how beautiful their children would be?"

"We don't even know that anything happened between them," Reese corrected. The last thing Masey needed was rumors flying. "Let's not marry them off just yet, okay?"

Trish shrugged then caught sight of Halie. "The place is gorgeous," she squealed, leaving Reese and Ben to greet her friend.

"Did I show you what I was going to do with the kitchen?" Ben whispered in Reese's ear. They were alone now, so she wasn't sure why he was whispering, but it felt good to have him stand so close, have his hot breath run against her ear.

"Why don't you refresh my memory?"

She led him down the dark hall.

He pulled her through the swinging door and into the dimly lit gourmet kitchen. Evening light slanted in the windows lighting up an old commercial-grade stove and stainless steel countertops.

Ben pressed her against a wall and kissed her. It was a good kiss. Patient. Soft. Slow. Thorough. But the longer his mouth was on hers, the less patient he became. His hands had found the hem of her dress.

"Party," she reminded him on a moan, but even as she said it, she found her legs parting, making room for his hand to explore what was under her dress.

His hand crept further north and he groaned.

Make that what *wasn't* under her dress.

"They won't miss us," he said, his mouth against her neck.

"Reese, you in here?" Luke said, pushing through the doors as if on cue. He spotted them then spun around, giving them his back. "Come on, you guys."

Reese bit her lip.

"What'd you need, Luke?" Ben asked.

"Halie wanted Reese out front," he grumbled, then pushed back through the door. "Can't keep their hands off each other for five minutes."

Reese sighed. "I think we're starting to annoy our friends."

Ben nibbled at her neck and stroked between her legs until she gasped. "They're just jealous."

"I need to get out front, though," she said, shimmying away from him.

He groaned and held her fast. "Did I mention that I'd be working this job for months? That's a lot of lunch breaks."

"Think you might need some company for any of those?"

He slid his hands down her back and hauled her up against him so she could feel his erection. "A lot. I get lonely, you know."

"Hmm," she said against his lips. "I'm not sure how Halie would feel about us *having lunch* all over her house."

"Well, it is her fault we're like this."

"I guess if you look at it that way…" She wrapped her arms around his neck and kissed him. Down the hall, the click of heels sounded, coming closer.

"Reese, do you know where the rest of the crystal wine glasses are?" Halie called.

Reese ignored her boss and slid her hands into Ben's hair.

The swinging door squeaked as it opened again. "Oh, you two," Halie said. "Never mind."

Another squeak and they were alone.

"Told you she wouldn't care," Ben murmured against her lips. "I think you're her favorite success story."

"I didn't change all that much," Reese protested.

"You and I know that," Ben said with a shrug. "I would like you to change one little thing about yourself for me, though."

Reese stepped back and crossed her arms. "Tread carefully, mister."

He took her hand. "Wear this for me."

Reese felt the cool metal of the ring before she saw the diamond-encrusted band. "Oh."

"Marry me, Reese," Ben said, his green eyes crinkling in the corners. "Let's commit our lives to making our friends jealous and nauseating our relatives."

She ran her hand over his jaw, his scruffy cheeks, her chest tight with happiness. "You promise to assist me in any crazy Sex Goddess training my boss sends me through?"

"If I must." He knotted his hands in her hair and studied her. "I love you, Reese."

"I love you too, Ben."

"You haven't said *yes* yet."

"I'm gonna make you sweat it," she said. "Someone taught me all about delayed gratification."

He growled. "He was an idiot."

"Hey, watch how you talk about my fiancé."

THE END

AVAILABLE NOW BY LEXI RYAN...

TEXT APPEAL

CHAPTER ONE

"Hello, my name is Riley, and I am addicted to sexy lingerie." Riley Carter steeled herself to walk past Fredrick's of Hollywood without spending next week's paycheck. She kept her stride long and even, moving along with the Miracle Mile crowd in the oppressive Las Vegas heat. With every step, disappointment crushed her internal lingerie junkie.

"Keep moving, Riley," she told herself. But then she made a tactical error. She glanced at the store's window and saw four big red letters dooming her to a month of tap water and peanut butter sandwiches: SALE.

The mother ship was calling her home.

Riley peeked over each shoulder, scanning the crowd for familiar faces before tucking her head and making a sharp right into the store.

"Senorita Carter," Javier, the doorman, said as she entered the store. "We've missed you. Where've you been?"

Heat blasted her cheeks. She'd failed in her attempts to break her slightly naughty and very secret little addiction. She had made some progress, though. It had been twenty-six days, two hours and—she glanced at her watch—five minutes since she'd fed her inner vixen. In that time, she hadn't bought a single bustier, teddy, or lacey panty. "It hasn't been that long," she said, but it had felt like an eternity. So what? She had a lingerie addiction. She lived in Sin City, where people came to feed old addictions—and find new ones. In comparison, lingerie was harmless—though an old-fashioned crack habit might have been cheaper.

"Big sale today," Javier was saying, but she'd already zeroed in on the sale racks, mentally calculating her budget.

To her right, a mannequin wore a black leather bustier with red piping and matching corset laces—not a sale item. She wondered if Chaz would approve of it—or of any of the hundreds of naughty-but-never-worn items in her collection. She imagined the leather hugging the underside of her breasts, leaving the tops exposed. She had a pair of red stilettos that would look fabulous with—

Focus, Riley!

She narrowed in on the deep discount sale bins. Thirty seconds later, she was elbow deep in thongs, garter belts and crotchless panties.

She studied a vibrant pink pair of the latter and bit her lip. Though her collection would put the famed Victoria and all of her secrets to shame, she'd yet to indulge in this particular variety of naughtiness. What was the point? Crotchless panties were for women who had illicit rendezvous in restaurant bathrooms or the backs of limos. They were for women whose boyfriends were so hot for them they couldn't wait the two-point-five seconds required for panty removal.

In short, they were for hoo-haws that saw more sex than a hotel room above a twenty-four-hour wedding chapel on the Strip.

Riley sighed and fingered the lace tie at the panty's hip. A smile curved her lips as she remembered the text Chaz sent her that morning.

I miss you. Are you available for dinner?

She hadn't gotten a chance to answer him before her cell had gone missing. Chaz was the kind of guy she'd always wanted. He was courteous and gracious, and her father loved him. Like Riley, Chaz worked for her father's empire: Carter Hotels and Entertainment. He understood the demands of the business.

"Black lace would be a better contrast against your fair skin," someone said behind her.

Riley jumped and dropped the panties. Cheeks ablaze, she looked up.

"But I like the style. I could definitely see you in something like that." Charlie Singleton—the face of professional poker—stood before her wearing Ray-Bans and a come-hither smile that made her insides do a little Snoopy dance. Eyes concealed by his ever-present shades, the only sign of his approving once-over was slight tilt of his head and the Machiavellian smile twisting his lips. Damn it all, but he made her skin tingle.

Riley's Inner Naughty Girl practically purred. *Charlie would like the black leather bustier.*

Of course he would. Charlie liked women—in clothes, in lingerie, out of clothes, out of lingerie. From what she'd seen, he didn't discriminate. Heck, he probably made eyes at the old ladies who took up residence in front of the slots at the Bellagio. It was his special talent. He made every woman feel like the only one in the room. Or, at least, the only one who mattered.

"I'm just...I'm just picking something up for my friend," she stammered.

Charlie's broad chest shook with his silent laugh. "Isn't that the excuse I'm supposed to use?"

Riley pulled her shoulders back and stuck out her chin. "No, I don't imagine you'd use an excuse at all. Instead, you'd tell me that you were looking for something skimpy for your latest supermodel conquest. Then you'd probably try to get me to help you pick it out."

He cocked his head, thoughtful, then, with a shrug, nodded. "I guess that's a fair assessment. So, we've covered that I'm only here because I'm a womanizing cad." His smile let her know he wasn't displeased by the conclusion. "What about you? Is this a secret side of Riley I've been missing out on?"

Good gracious! She needed Charlie Singleton knowing about her lingerie addiction like she needed a hole in the head.

With a sigh, Riley snuck a glance at the pink panties she'd dropped into the bin. Damn, Charlie! She was going to have to walk away empty-handed now. Her Inner Naughty Girl whimpered.

She shot Charlie a glare she hoped was withering.

He shook his head and pulled off his sunglasses, giving her a full view of his rarely-revealed ice blue eyes. She wished he'd put them back on.

Charlie had this unsettling habit of looking at her like she was a triple chocolate ice cream cone with a single drip running down the side—a look that worried her as much as it turned her on.

"I'm glad to see you, Riley," he said, flashing that signature smile again. "I've been thinking about you." He eyed the discount bin. "And I can't say I mind the circumstances."

She nodded, pretending that smile didn't turn her insides to goo, pretending part of her hadn't been counting down the days until next week's thirtieth annual Grand Escape Resort and Casino's National Poker Tournament. Since her father's hotel hosted the tournament, it meant guaranteed face time with Mr. Two Scoop Sundae.

She liked to look at Charlie. She liked the way he looked at her. Liked the way her belly flip-flopped when he entered a room. What was the harm in that? It wasn't as though she planned to *do* anything about it.

"Have you seen your sister yet?" she asked, groping for a subject safer than lingerie or even why he might have been thinking about her. Riley's roommate, Lacey, was Charlie's sister. Charlie had moved to L.A. as a teen and still kept a home there, but he was in Vegas often enough for poker tournaments that he and his sister remained close.

Charlie shook his head. "Just got in."

And Fredrick's was his first stop? Further evidence that Charlie was capital B, capital N, Bad News. Riley sighed and stole a final glance at the panties. *Adieu, my friend. We could have been great together.* "Well, I'll let her know. I lost my phone this morning and she's meeting me to help me pick out a new one." In fact, she was supposed to be on her way right now. *Not* shopping for lingerie with Charlie No-Other-Man-Will-Ever-Measure-Up Singleton.

Charlie looped his finger under the ribbon of the panties he'd caught Riley holding. He lifted them from the bin. "On second thought," he murmured, "the vibrant pink would look good with your dark hair."

Riley covered her face. "Oh. My. God. You did not just say that."

"What?" He pulled away her hand.

"I don't want you thinking about my hair *down there*," she whispered.

Charlie chuckled. "Who said anything about *down there*?" He shifted his gaze to the panties and, upon spotting their special feature, broadened his smile. "Well, I'll be damned. You're a little kinky, aren't you?"

She slapped at his hand, trying to make him drop the offending panties. "They're not for me," she seethed. "I have a friend who...who..." What? Had a medical need for crotchless panties? Bluffing had never been Riley's strength. "She's getting married."

He cocked a brow. "Honey, married women don't wear panties like these. These are reserved for wild single chicks, or..." He studied her for a beat. Raised a brow. "...good girls with a secret naughty side?"

One of the saleswomen approached. "How are you today, Miss Carter? Is there anything we can get for you?"

Riley cringed. She wanted to peek at Charlie—did he notice the saleswoman calling her by name?—but she was too nervous. There were plenty of reasons they might know her...

"I saw you noticing the black leather bustier," the woman continued. "I'll be honest, I thought of you when it came in. I thought, 'Miss Carter would just *swoon* for this!' And I was right, wasn't I? We even have a matching red leather thong. I tucked back a set in your size so we wouldn't sell out before you made it in. I know how you like me to do that."

"Um..." Riley wished she could disappear. "No, thanks, I don't think that's what I'll be getting my *friend*." She risked a glance at Charlie.

The saleswoman frowned.

Charlie was studying Riley now, but at least that damn smirk was gone. "She'll take it," he said, never taking his eyes off Riley's face.

The saleswoman's smile returned. "Great," she said before bouncing away.

"I'm not going to let you buy me lingerie, Charlie," Riley said, but her eyes were glued to the bustier on display, and Inner Naughty Girl was damn near salivating over the thought of her next fix.

Time she accept the facts: if she was going to kick this addiction, she needed professional help—something she should have recognized around the time she'd nicknamed her secret wild side her ING.

"Don't be a spoil sport, Ry," Charlie said, his voice soft.

Riley chewed on her lip and tore her eyes away from the bustier to look at Charlie. ING purred again. Apparently she liked Charlie even more than she liked lingerie—precisely why she couldn't be trusted.

"I see the way you look at that bustier."

"It's fine leather craftsmanship," she said, forcing a shrug. "I appreciate the work."

With a smile, he lowered his voice. "Honey, look at me like you're looking at that get-up, and I'll buy you the whole damn store." He winked and her insides shimmied.

The rational part of her brain stepped forward, and she thumped him on the arm. "Stop coming on to me."

He cocked his head. "Why?"

"Because I'm..." That was a good question. Why?

Right. Chaz. *Remember Chaz*, she lectured herself. "I'm seeing someone."

"Ah," Charlie said, sliding his glasses back on and hiding

those hypnotic blue eyes. "And you don't want to be thinking of me when you wear it for him?"

"No!"

"You won't think of me?"

"I won't wear it for him," she said through her teeth.

He raised a brow. "Because...he prefers satin?"

"I'm not going to wear it at all," she seethed. "Chaz doesn't need me to dress in outrageous lingerie. He's very...respectable."

Charlie wrinkled his nose. "I'm sorry. Do you want me to talk to him about that?"

"Why would I—? No!" Why did she always let him do this to her? All he had to do was walk in a room and she turned into a frazzled, driveling idiot.

And—more to the point—why did she seem to *enjoy* it?

Charlie strode to the counter where the saleswoman was ringing up the bustier.

Riley swallowed. She could practically feel the leather now. What would it hurt, really, letting him buy her a little something? They were friends. Wasn't that what friends did?

Where was her reasonable self when she needed her?

You left her out on the sidewalk, Riley, right next to your dignity.

***

I hope you enjoyed this sample of *Text Appeal—Available now!*

ABOUT THE AUTHOR

Author of both contemporary and paranormal romance, Lexi Ryan writes smart, spunky stories that sizzle. She enjoys reading, sunshine, a good glass of wine, and rare trips to the beach with her husband and children.

Lexi lives in Indiana where she divides her time between her family, her writing, and her social media addiction. She loves hearing from readers, so don't hesitate to send her an email or find her on facebook or Twitter!

To sign up for her newsletter or learn about new releases, visit Lexi on her website: lexiryan.com